Slipperless Series

(Book #3)

By Sloan Storm

This is a work of fiction. Names, places, businesses, characters and incidents are either the product of the author's imagination or are used in a fictitious manner. Any resemblance to actual persons living or dead, actual events or locales is purely coincidental.

FIONA

I ran my fingers through my hair, shaking them free with a vigorous motion.

Afterward, I reached for my third cup of coffee and tilted it up to my mouth, finishing it with a thick swallow.

The silky texture of cream combined with the sweet hint of sugar across my tongue were subtle reminders of the effect the caffeine had on my nervous system.

As I finished it off, I placed my empty mug down on my workstation and went to grab my pen, when I noticed it for the first time. My hand shook as it hovered just above the desk's surface. Undaunted, I balled my fingers into a fist, straightened myself up in my chair and snatched it. Pinching the hard plastic between my fingertips, I pressed the pen's tip against the page with focus.

I licked my lips and began to scribble my notes once more, determined this time to not allow distractions to creep in and disrupt me. I still had a bit of time before the staff arrived, and so while I had the chance to catch up, I needed to make the most of it. I'd been trying to keep focused on the long list of tasks in my planner. However, I found I couldn't manage more than about ten minutes or so of dedicated concentration before my mind wandered to my troubles.

The irony was, of course, that my job at Hawkins Biotech was supposed to solve my problems, not create a half dozen more.

I spent an entire weekend obsessing over my last encounter with Gabe and the potential damage it was doing to my career, as well as my life. I hadn't been eating much and sleeping even less. My grandmother took notice even as I did my best to conceal it from her. When she asked, I lied and told her I was under stress from finishing the lab work and the upcoming presentation I was scheduled to make. She'd been so out of it over the weekend, it seemed as if she believed me.

That was a good thing, because time was running out on my charade.

I glanced up around the still-empty lab. At this point, I had to take silver linings where I could get them and when it came to the staff, I'd managed a small one. Since my meeting with the team, things had improved for the better.

Although productivity was down a little, morale was up and it looked as if, for the moment anyway, Amanda and Melissa's attempt at a coup was put to rest. A big part of the reason for that was, so far, I'd managed to keep my involvement with Gabe to little more than petty gossip between the two women. While I was sure they'd done their part to try and spread it as best they could, it hadn't had the desired effect.

At least, not yet.

With respect to the presentation, I'd gone to a couple of local Toastmasters meetings to learn how to be an effective communicator. The simple fact was that I knew the material about the Link Protocol as well as could be expected. Now it was just a matter of overcoming my fears.

Unfortunately, my first couple of speeches at Toastmasters hadn't gone well. I was ten—no—a *hundred* times more nervous than I anticipated. And although I didn't yet know exactly when I was to give the presentation, based on where we were in the project, I figured it wouldn't be long.

So even though things with work were going all right, the same couldn't be said about what was going on with Gabe. I began to feel less and less able to turn him away when it came to sex. This was partially due to the fact that I wasn't altogether sure he wouldn't fire me if I didn't sleep with him. Also, well, because I began to feel like I couldn't.

Nothing could have prepared me for what happened to me in his office the last time we were together. On the one hand, the way he'd treated me left me feeling something close to humiliated. On the other, what he'd done stimulated and excited me in a way I can't explain.

I racked my brain, trying to sort through the confusing thoughts and emotions in the silence of my bedroom at home. But after two long days and much longer nights, I wasn't any closer to understanding the changes taking place inside me, brought about by him. They were frightening and liberating at the same time. I found myself in unfamiliar territory with no clear path forward. All my life, I'd relied on my rationality and reason to guide me, teach me, tell me…

What I ought to do.

What I should study.

What I need to say.

Yet, in his office, under his control, I felt free in a way I hadn't before. My intellect failed me. There was nothing, not a single thing, about what he did that would appeal to reason. In fact, it should have been the exact opposite. I should have been appalled at what he'd done—outraged. After all, look at how he'd treated me...

He commanded me.

He ordered me.

He owned me.

But ironically, far from being repulsed by it, the simple truth was I'd never felt *more feminine* in my entire life. For once, for just a few moments, I wasn't the one responsible. I didn't have to care for anyone, answer to anyone or tell anyone what to do. Of all places, it was on his desk, being taken by him in the most primitive way imaginable, that I realized true bliss. And I'm not just talking about my orgasm. I began to feel as though there was something liberating about giving away my power to have to choose, to make a decision.

Unfortunately, as much as it thrilled me, the consequences of being found out would have the exact opposite effect. With each day that passed, I grew more certain my co-workers would find out about what was happening between us. For his part, Gabe seemed unconcerned about such an outcome. He'd put me in an impossible situation and the worst part of it was, some twisted part of me enjoyed it.

I took a break from my writing, and as I did, I felt my hand shake once again, far worse than it had before. Around the same time, a feeling of lightheadedness overcame me. Whether it was too much sugar, lack of sleep, or both, I had the sensation I might faint. I felt my skin go moist as clammy perspiration coated my forehead and the back of my neck.

"Oh please, no," I whispered, as I laid my head down on my desk.

I had to get out of the office. I couldn't risk anyone seeing me like this.

Not now.

GABE

After lunch the following Tuesday, I'd just wrapped a conference call with a group of investors. It had been a long few days since the last time I'd slept with Fiona. I'd thoroughly enjoyed the last encounter. As a result, I had every reason to suspect she'd come around to my way of thinking.

And speaking of that, I'd made arrangements for her to come to my office and give me a report on the progress in the lab, as well as the presentation. As much as I would like to for her visit to be more than business, there wasn't any time for it today. In fact, there was scarcely time for her update. Yet, it had to get done, and done as soon as possible, since there was precious little time to waste. After hanging up from the call, I pressed the intercom button.

"Holly, is Fiona out there?"

After a brief pause, she replied. "No, Gabe, she isn't."

I scowled as I leaned forward in my chair. Glaring in the direction of the phone I continued, "She's not? Where in the hell is she? I told you to get her up here."

Holly didn't hesitate as she responded. "Oh, I tried. Believe me. I called down to the lab, but she's gone."

"Gone? Where did she go?"

"Apparently she wasn't feeling well and went home."

I reached up and wiped my palm down the length of my face. "Are you serious?"

"Mmm, hmm. I confirmed it with Colin," Holly murmured. "I was waiting until you got off your conference call, and I was going to let you know. Um, would you like me to try and reach her?"

I couldn't believe it. "Yes, right away."

"O-Okay," Holly began. "I'll take care of it."

"Good. Thanks Holly… If you get a hold of Fiona, put her through to me."

"All right. Anything else or…"

As Holly spoke, I couldn't help but think about how bizarre this behavior was for Fiona. She wasn't the type to leave work. When she had her fainting episode before, she hadn't left then, so what the hell was the difference this time?

I couldn't explain it, but I had this gnawing feeling she still wasn't fucking getting how critical the situation was with the Link Protocol. Apparently, I hadn't made my displeasure with her clear enough in my office Friday night. I stood from my chair and raked my fingers through my hair.

"You know what, Holly?"

"Yes?"

"Forget the call. Get my limo ready. I'm going over there myself."

Holly hesitated for a moment. "Oh… Well okay. Are you sure? I don't mind calling. It's not a…"

"Yes," I replied, cutting her off. "I'm one hundred percent sure. I'll be downstairs in ten minutes. Give Tomas the address to Fiona's place."

"Okay, Gabe. I will. Right away."

"Thanks, sweetheart."

Fifteen minutes later, I was nearly halfway to Fiona's when I decided to call her. Sliding my hand inside my jacket,

I ran my fingers along the smooth silk interior. I reached inside the pocket, wrapped my fingers around the hard plastic and pulled it out. Seconds later, the line connected and rang a couple of times before going straight to her voice mail. Glancing out the window at the blurred landscape as it passed by, I disconnected the call without leaving a message and dropped my hand to my lap in disgust.

Not a lot of things get me upset. Over the years, I'd developed a pretty thick skin when it came to dealing with people and their flaky behavior, especially women. Collecting myself, I leaned back into the seat, straightened my tie and my jacket. Until I could get her face-to-face and understand just what the hell was going on, gritting my teeth over this wasn't going to help me.

Yet, I also understood the precariousness of the situation I'd gotten myself into by relying on her to do the presentation. Fiona was going to have to find a way to put all the distractions aside and focus. If she did what I asked of her, all of her financial problems would vanish in an instant.

As for our involvement, well, if she couldn't find a way to keep business and pleasure separate, I'd put a stop to it if need be. That's not what I wanted to do. She was a helluva piece of ass. A great fucking lay. Just the thought of being inside her threatened to get my cock hard as stone—but one way or another, she'd have to understand the urgency of this situation.

Soon my attention returned to the city scene beyond the tinted glass in the back seat of the limo. I didn't recognize anything about the surroundings, but from the looks of it, we'd driven to one of the shittier parts of town, if not the shittiest. Just then, Tomas slowed the limo and pulled into the parking lot of a dilapidated apartment complex. I jostled about in the backseat as the vehicle dipped into potholes and rolled over speed bumps that looked as if they'd been jackhammered into huge chunks.

As we meandered through the parking lot, everything I laid my eyes on appeared to have suffered from years of neglect. The entire place was in a state of total disrepair. The city could come through and condemn the whole damn place and I doubted anyone would raise an eyebrow.

Driving deeper into the complex, things got worse… an empty swimming pool, now filled with trash and weeds. Turning a corner, a large, run down playground with broken swings and a basketball court with no hoops came into view. I reached for the divider window control. The thick glass whined as it descended. When it reached the halfway position, I stopped it.

"Tomas," I began, as I looked at him in the rear view mirror. "Are you sure this is the right place?"

His eyes locked on mine in the reflection "Yes, sir, Mr. Hawkins. It's the address Miss Holly gave me. Miss Matthews' building, sir. Straight ahead."

"All right, pull up and park. I won't be long."

"Yes, sir."

With that, I rolled the window back up once more and readied myself for the scene I was likely to encounter. It'd been a long time since I was broke, but I remembered what it was like.

It fucking sucked.

But at least in my case the poverty stemmed from trying to build my business. As soon as I did, my money problems disappeared in an instant. Fiona had it way worse since the reason she was broke had nothing to do with entrepreneurial zeal, but rather her goodwill.

The simple fact was that when you're more than a half a million in debt, it severely limits your housing options. Difficult though she was, I respected the hell out of her tenacity. It's not every early twenty-something you meet who had the guts to take on debt like that.

It said something remarkable about her character.

It was a helluva situation, with two distinct parts to it. First, what the situation required with her was a stern hand. I had no problem with that aspect of it. The other half though—it was a bit more difficult. In the midst of everything going on with billion dollar deals, it's easy to lose sight of your employees' real life struggles.

And leaving aside whatever had happened between Fiona and me so far, the fact was that she was still my employee.

Just then, the limo came a stop.

Tomas got out and opened the door. As it cracked open, the back seat filled with bright white from the afternoon sun. I reached for the limo door, hooking my fingers around it, and as I exited, I glanced up towards Tomas.

"What apartment number is it?"

"4B, sir."

Within a few minutes, I stood in front of the door to Fiona's home. I had to block out the squalor as best I could. She and I still had some major issues to deal with. Shocking though her living situation was, I couldn't afford the distraction. After balling up my fist, I rapped against the door with my knuckles.

After ten seconds or so, and no response, I knocked a second time, only harder.

As before, nothing.

Biting my lip, I hardened my fist and with a series of rapid strikes, I pounded against the door with the fleshy pad of my hand. I hit it so hard, the door shook inside the frame. As I finished, I leaned in towards the door, listening for any hint of someone approaching.

Just then, it cracked open.

I leaned away as a chain stretched across the partially opened door caught my attention. Just above it, a pair of blue eyes, half-concealed in shadow stared back at me.

"Gabe," Fiona whispered. "What are you doing here?"

I frowned in disbelief. "What am *I* doing here? Why aren't *you* at work?"

Fiona turned her cheek, glancing away from me for a moment. She paused before looking back at me again. "You shouldn't have come here, Gabe."

"Open the door, Fiona."

She shook her head, shielding her eyes behind her hair. "No."

Without warning, Fiona made a sudden motion to close the door. As she did, I thrust my hand inside at the last instant, hooking it around the edge and stopping it in place. Fiona grunted as I forced her backward. The chain rattled as it flexed to its maximum.

"Gabe, stop it. Please."

"No," I replied. I shoved the door once more, stretching the links to their breaking point. "Let me in right now or you're fired, Fiona."

Fiona looked up at me through a curious gaze. If I didn't know any better, I'd say her eyes held the reflection of shame in them.

"Gabe, please don't. Look, I-I'll come outside to talk to you. Okay?"

Still holding the door with a forceful grasp, I felt the tension ease from her body through the door as she stopped resisting me. I studied her for a moment or so before I answered at last.

"All right," I said, nodding. "Come on out."

Fiona's gaze remained fixed on me as I accepted her bargain. I peeled my fingers away from the door, and as I did, she lowered her head and disappeared from view while she closed the door. I heard the distinctive sound of the chain as it rattled free. A moment later, Fiona cracked the door open, pulling it inward towards her. As she did, I wasted no time and pushed against it. In less than a second, I'd crossed the threshold into her apartment.

"You bastard!" she said with a loud whisper. Fiona pressed her small palms into my chest, slapping me and shoving me as I walked inside. "You promised!"

I grunted as her harmless blows glanced off my torso. Just then, Fiona turned away from me and grabbed hold of the doorknob once again. She gestured towards the yellow daylight beyond the entrance.

"Get out Gabe, get out, get out!"

I glared at her in silence. "I'm not leaving, Fiona. I'm not going anywhere until you tell me what the hell is going on with you."

After I issued my warning, I took a quick look around. Man, she lived in borderline poverty. And the apartment itself was barely big enough for one person, let alone two. I'd assumed her grandmother lived with her but I didn't see or hear anything to indicate where she might be.

"Gabe!" Fiona said, stomping her foot. "Leave! Now!"

Ignoring her, I continued to study the surroundings in complete disbelief. Even at my poorest, I never lived anywhere this run down. As I gazed in slack-jawed wonder, Fiona reached her boiling point and slammed the front door. She marched over towards me, and grabbed hold of my arm at the bicep. As she did, I heard something down the hallway. Without thinking, I nearly asked about her grandmother but at the last second, I caught myself.

Instead, I nodded in the direction of the sound. "Left your television on."

Fiona snapped her hands to her hips. "Thank you for the update. Will you please leave?"

I nodded. "Yeah, okay, Fiona. I'll go. But before I do, you're going to tell me what the hell is going on with you or I can promise you won't have a job to come back to."

She thinned her lips and spun in a flash, turning her back to me. In the span of a few seconds, Fiona disappeared into the kitchen. I followed right behind, the soles of my shoes sinking into the old, soft linoleum flooring. At one point, it felt as if they might give way and I'd fall straight through to the apartment below.

Fiona stopped and with her back still facing me, she reached up and ran both of her hands through her hair. Afterward, she placed them flat on the counter, just at the edge of the partially rusted aluminum sink. Fiona locked her arms straight, dropping her head a bit.

"What do you want from me, Gabe?"

I reached up towards my face and wiped my palm across my lips. "It's real simple, Fiona. I just want the truth."

"Gabe, I'm sorry I left the office, okay? I…"

I interrupted her. "Fiona I think I've given you ample opportunity to be honest with me. If you can't trust me enough to do that after everything I've offered to you well, then, I suppose there's nothing left to discuss."

With that, I turned to leave.

"Wait," Fiona called out as I walked away. "Where are you going?"

I stopped in place and turned to face her once again. "What do you mean, Fiona? Back to the office. Where else?"

Fiona's shoulders slumped. "Oh, okay."

"So that's it then?" I replied in disbelief. "You're just going to give up? Not fight for any of this?"

She shook her head with a listless rhythm. "I'm not sure I can anymore."

"Well, then I've heard all I need to hear. Goodbye Fiona. And good luck. You're gonna need it."

I'd made a few steps closer to the front door when I heard Fiona close on me from behind. "Gabe, wait. Please."

With my fingers wrapped around the dented, cold brass knob, I paused. "What?"

"Promise me you won't be upset."

"No, Fiona. I won't promise that," I began, as I released the knob from my grasp and turned around to face her. I gestured with both arms, spreading them wide. "Is this how you want to live your life? Look at this place… What is it you're so afraid of you aren't willing to take whatever risk you must to get out of here?"

"It's not that simple, Gabe. You don't understand."

"Well, then you need to explain it to me, Fiona because you're right. At this point, I absolutely do not understand. I'm giving you an opportunity that one hundred percent of people in your position would kill to have. But, seemingly every time I turn around, you give in to the pressure with unexplained illness. Tell me, what would you think if you were me? How would you act?"

Fiona broke her gaze upon me and as she did, I noticed her eyes glaze over with a tell-tale sign.

"You're right, okay?" she said with a nod. Her tone carried genuine sadness. "The stress of all of it. The position of team leader, the presentation, us…"

I had to admit, seeing her like that didn't sit well with me. Not one bit. But pressure is something that everyone deals with in one form or another. It's part of life. How I felt about it, one way or the other, didn't really matter.

"Fiona," I said, as I stepped towards her and cradled her upper arms with my hands. "You know I want to help you and see you succeed. You do believe me don't you?"

Fiona nodded in agreement. "Yes."

"Some of what I do probably seems a bit excessive at times, but it's only because I have such high standards for you. I believe in you and I think you have an awful lot to contribute to the company."

"Thank you. I'm sorry."

I waved her off. I had no time or use for self-pity.

"I need you back at the office, Fiona. You need to find the strength from somewhere to go back. And I don't mean a week from now, I mean this afternoon. Is that clear?"

She nodded.

FIONA

Just as I closed the front door, my grandmother called for me from her bedroom. I made my way down the hall, and as I entered, I looked in her direction.

"I think the battery died," she grumbled. Clutching a pair of noise cancelling headphones I recently purchased for her in her hand, she held them up, pointing them in my direction. "Can you see if there's something wrong with them? I'm missing my show. I unplugged them but I can't hear a darn thing."

In recent months it had become more and more difficult for her to hear the television, unless I turned the volume up to a level far too loud for my liking. As a compromise, I'd purchased the headphones for her a couple of weeks earlier.

After taking them from her hand, I turned them to one side and noticed the battery indicator light was indeed off. I stifled a lump in my throat. Hard of hearing though she was, I couldn't be certain she hadn't heard Gabe and me. After all, he'd heard the television after she'd unplugged the headphones. I wasn't concerned she would have heard the details of the conversation but the sound of a man's voice would result in questions.

"It's the battery, Grandmother," I said, as I pointed at the indicator light. "Do you remember? If it's not blue, then the battery needs to be replaced."

She nodded. "Oh yes, that's right. I'm sorry about that, dear."

"It's okay, I'll get some more batteries from the kitchen and bring them in here so you can keep them next to your bed."

"Thank you, Fiona."

I smiled and turned to walk away, thankful that my concerns about whether or not she heard us were wrong. I made it almost all the way across the room but just as I reached the threshold of the doorway, she spoke once more.

"Oh and dear, when you come back, you can tell me all about it."

I stopped and did a half-turn in her direction. Frowning, I replied, "All about what?"

"The man you were talking to by the front door. It wasn't Charlie's voice—that much is for certain."

Charlie was the maintenance man for the apartment complex. The building was so old that hardly a week or two went by without him coming by to repair something. I swallowed, but did my best not to seem bothered by her demand. "Oh, that. It was nothing."

My grandmother cocked her head and staring at me beneath a wrinkled brow she said, "Now Fiona, you know full well I'm not going to accept that from you."

I pinched the inside of my cheek between my teeth for a moment. "Well… what did you want to know?"

"For starters? Who was it?"

"Grandmother, I've got to get back to the office. Now, let me get your batteries and I'll be right back."

"No, Fiona," she said, as she lifted her arm and wagged her index finger at me. "Who was it?"

Clutching the headphones, I traced my index finger along the soft leather earcups. "It was my boss, Gabe."

She paused for a moment and looked at me in confusion. Before she had a chance to say anything, I turned to leave as fast as I could.

"Look, I'm gonna go get a battery for your headphones and…"

"No!" she exclaimed. "Fiona Matthews, you will do no such thing!"

I shook my head as I backed away. "I don't want to talk about this, okay? I have to get back to the office, Grandmother. Please."

She ignored me, and before I realized it, the questioning began in earnest. "So that's why he came here? To get you back to work?"

I looked down, tugging my shirt down around my curves. Afterward, I drew my hands together in front of my body, holding the headphones as I did.

"Fiona?"

"What?" I began, as I locked eyes with her. "What do you want me to say? Yes, he came to find out what was going on and to get me back into the office. All right?"

"There's no need to get snippy with me, Fiona," she said, as she placed her hands in her lap.

"I'm sorry."

She nodded, but I could tell her line of questioning was far from complete. My grandmother narrowed her eyes at me. "Tell me this. Since when does the CEO of a big company make a personal visit to an employee's house to check on their well-being?"

I exhaled. "What do you want me to tell you, Grandmother?"

"The truth, Fiona. You've been vague and mysterious about him all along. But now this man is coming into our home. There's more to this, and I want you to tell me now. I deserve that much from you."

"Grandmother, believe me. I'm not trying to keep anything from you. It's just… I don't want you to worry. I can handle it okay?"

"Well, now I am worried, Fiona. This is a disaster in the making. You should stop whatever is happening before it's too late and it affects your career. Heaven forbid you get involved with him. That would be a dreadful mistake."

"What do you mean?"

"Fiona, don't pretend you don't know what I mean. You know exactly what I'm talking about. You're a grown woman now. A man only does things like he's doing when he's interested in one thing and one thing only."

I looked away from her for a moment, curling the sleeves of my shirt in my fingers.

"You weren't honest with me about the dinner you had with him, Fiona. I have to tell you that hurts my feelings."

"I know, I'm sorry. I wasn't trying to keep it from you. You've not been well. That's all."

"No. I know you don't like it when I tell you this, but you're young and there's some things in life you don't know about yet. This is one of those things. It's really for the best if you end this Fiona, before it goes any further."

What could I say? There was no way I could tell her what was going on. Even worse, what she said made a lot of sense. It was hard to disagree with her logic.

Nodding, I looked at her once more. "You're right, Grandmother. I'd have to be a fool not to see it."

Her face brightened a bit at my agreement. "I'm sorry to be the one to have to tell you this, Fiona. It really is for the best though."

"Okay," I began with a solemn nod. "All right. I'll do something about it. I promise. I'm going to go get your batteries now."

"Okay, dear."

I turned, left the room and walked towards the kitchen. As I did, I found myself struggling against now familiar emotions. Intellectually, rationally, I understood and agreed with everything she said. I had no good reason to think that continuing with Gabe would result in anything but problems for me. After all, he came to my home. What was next? To what lengths would he go to have me do as he wished?

But then there was the other part of me. The part that had all but lost the ability to resist him any longer. I worried that if he were to send for me, demanding I come to his office, I wouldn't be able to deny him whatever he wanted from me.

But I couldn't tell my Grandmother that. That struggle was one I'd have to endure alone.

GABE

Fiona had returned to work, and except for the few hours she'd disappeared, she hadn't missed a beat. As much as I would have liked to get to the bottom of whatever was going on with her, I didn't have the time. She was just going to have to work through this on her own for now. And frankly, after getting a bit of distance from the situation, I realized that was the best thing for her.

A couple of days had passed since I went to her apartment. We hadn't spoken, but even so, I still needed the updates she'd avoided giving me. It was the first time since then I had a few minutes to spare. Picking up the phone, I dialed Holly to have her get Fiona to my office as soon as possible. She must have stepped out, because after a few rings, there was still no answer. With no time to waste, I disconnected and called Fiona myself.

She picked up after the second ring.

"Fiona, I need you to come to my office."

She remained silent for a moment. Through the receiver, I detected the sound of a swallow just before she spoke. "Do I have to?"

Pulling the phone away, I glanced at it in disbelief for a moment before returning it to my ear. "Yes, Fiona. You do."

More discomfort sputtered from her lips. "Couldn't we just handle it over the phone? I'm happy to tell you whatever it is you want to know."

I wrapped my hand around the receiver, crushing it in my grip. I gathered myself, taking a moment before I continued. "Fiona… If I wanted to handle it over the phone, I wouldn't tell you to come to my office, now would I? What exactly is the problem?"

"There isn't one. I-I'll be up as soon as I can."

"Now. Not five minutes from now. Or an hour. Right now. Drop whatever it is you're doing, and come at once."

"Okay, I…"

I slammed the phone down in its cradle as she muttered, disconnecting her. Afterward, I shot to my feet. Sliding my hand through my hair, I took a few steps around my desk and tried to calm myself ahead of her arrival. About ten minutes later, the intercom on my phone crackled to life. The sound of Holly's voice interrupted my train of thought as I sat at my desk going over some clinical trial data we'd received on the Link Protocol.

"Gabe," she began. "Fiona is here to see you."

"Okay, send her in."

Moments later, the door opened. Still too annoyed to look in her direction, I continued to peruse my notes and pointed in the direction of the conference table.

"Have a seat, Fiona."

She closed the door, and I listened as she crossed the room and slid into one of the chairs. After a deep inhale, I stood from mine and walked in her direction. Fiona sat at the table, both hands on it with her fingers interlocked. As I drew near, she looked up at me. I noticed a slight clench of her jaw as our eyes locked.

"Fiona, I don't have much time. We'll need to keep this brief."

She nodded as I paused.

"Not long ago, you sat in this office and told me you were ready to deliver the presentation to the investors."

Fiona shifted in her seat but never took her eyes off me as I spoke.

"That's right," she said, after a moment or two. Her tone carried a hint of false determination. It wasn't hard to see by the look in her eyes that she wasn't altogether sure of herself. Not only that, but if I wasn't mistaken, she seemed a bit... *annoyed*.

I gave her the benefit of the doubt for a moment. Circling around behind her, I continued, "Okay, well, we've not really had a chance to discuss it since that day. Are you still on track to do it?"

She shrugged as I finished my question.

"Fiona, I don't understand. I thought I made myself quite clear at your apartment. If you can't handle the pressure of the position or the presentation, I've got to know, and I've got to know right now."

Just then, Fiona raised her hand towards her mouth. This was not the time or the place for what I expected would follow.

"Don't start, Fiona."

She lowered her head, shielding her face behind her hair. I walked around to the opposite side of the table for a better look. While I moved, she turned her head once more. But as she did, I noticed a droplet splash on the surface of the table.

"Sorry," she muttered. Grasping her sleeves in her hand, she wiped at the lone tear, smearing it away with the fabric of her shirt.

I almost couldn't believe what I was witnessing. Frustrated with her behavior, I tried to encourage her nonetheless. "Fiona, you'll get through this. I promise you will."

She shook her head. "It's not that. I mean, I'm nervous about the presentation, but…"

I looked down at her as her voice trailed off. I shook my head. "But what, Fiona?"

Still not looking up at me, Fiona made two brief swipes at her cheeks before returning her hands to the top of the conference table.

"I-I don't know what to do anymore, Gabe," she said with a whisper. "I can't say 'no' to you."

Mystified, I slid one hand through my hair. "Fiona, why do you think you're here right now?"

She shrugged. "I'm not sure."

"What do you mean 'you're not sure'? I told you why I've summoned you here. I don't get the reason for the apprehension."

As I finished my thought, Fiona drew her eyes up to meet mine. The emotion that brought on the tears moments earlier appeared to have vanished. In its place, her irises flickered with a hint of anger.

"Do you have any idea, Gabe? What it's like? Being in my position?"

I exhaled in disbelief. Was she really serious?

"Fiona," I began with a groan. "Just tell me what you're getting at here."

"Never mind, it's nothing," she said with a casual flick of her hair. "I'll do whatever you tell me. What do you want me to do, Gabe?"

I leaned away as the meaning of her innuendo settled in upon me.

"Listen, Fiona. I asked you up here today strictly to discuss business matters. Nothing more."

"Yet somehow it always winds up as something more, doesn't it, Gabe?"

I crossed my arms at my chest. After glaring in silence for a moment or two, I replied, "There's a lot of women who'd like to trade places with you. Believe me."

"Well, I wish they would."

Wiping my hand over my mouth, I took a few steps towards the conference table. As I reached it, I leaned over it and placed both palms flat.

"You act like… I'm a monster or something, Fiona," I began. I shook my head and with a shrug added, "Look, if you don't want to have sex, I'm not going to force it on you. Frankly, I really resent the fucking attitude. I've given you a goddamn lot since you've been here. Now I'm not gonna rehash everything we discussed at your apartment, but I will tell you this… So long as you work for me, you will do as I say. As far as the rest of it goes, well, you're free to tell me 'no'."

After I finished speaking, we looked at one another in silence for several moments. Eventually, Fiona broke her gaze.

"I'm only going to ask you once more, Fiona. How is the preparation going for the presentation? Have you been working on becoming a better speaker?"

After clearing her throat, Fiona spent the better part of the next five minutes explaining that she'd joined Toastmasters and was, in fact, growing in confidence where public speaking was concerned. Frustrated though I was with her, I listened intently, asking questions where I needed clarification. Satisfied she'd been putting in the effort she'd likely need, I nodded, returned to a standing position and walked back towards my desk.

"Thank you. Feel free to show yourself out, Fiona."

After a moment or two, I heard the sound of the chair moving along the carpet as she scooted it out from beneath the table. After sliding back into my own, I glanced up at her for a moment. As I did, Fiona smoothed her clothing and slid a handful of her blond hair behind her ears. It was a pity, really. She was such a beautiful woman. Curvy in all the right spots… an absolute angel. I just wished she'd learn to see herself the way I did.

"Gabe," she said, as she turned to leave. "I'm sorry. I- I didn't mean it."

Breaking eye contact with her, I reached for my pen. "Goodbye, Fiona. We've all got work to do. Let's get back to it."

FIONA

I stood there looking at him. My stomach sank.

All I wanted was for him not to treat me like an object at every opportunity he had. Of course it was flattering but at the same time it was becoming an ever greater threat to me in a professional and emotional sense. I couldn't understand why he was unable to see it.

The professional part of it had me less concerned. The presentation aside, I had enough confidence that the lab work and our contributions to the Link Protocol would be more than sufficient. And even though some hard deadlines were fast approaching, I didn't see any long term-risks to our progress.

On the other hand, the confidence I had in my emotions was far less reliable.

Obviously, my feelings for Gabe were far beyond what I'd ever experienced for a man. I still hadn't bothered to discuss them with anyone. When I was with him, even if not in a romantic sense, I felt safe. Yes, he challenged me in ways I never expected. Of course, it was difficult to go through change but far from resenting him for it, I did appreciate it.

And beyond that, deep down, in spite of his outward gruffness at times, I sensed Gabe was a good, caring person. Billions of dollars in net worth aside, only someone who truly cares about the well-being of other people would start a company like Hawkins Biotech.

Oh my God… What the hell am I doing?

Desperate not to leave things in an awkward, intense state between us yet again, I swallowed hard and prepared to clarify myself.

"Gabe… can I please say something?"

"Unless it has something to do with work, Fiona, I'm not interested."

"Well, it does."

Gabe made a few more strokes of the pen across the page and then stopped. After placing it down on the stack of paper in front of him, he folded his hands together and nodded.

"Go on."

I began to walk in the direction of his desk.

"May I sit?" I asked as I gestured towards one of the chairs across from him.

He nodded. "Yes, but make this quick."

I slid into the chair across from Gabe's desk. For a brief moment, I reached down to clutch my sleeves in my palms, but at the last instant, I resisted and cleared my throat.

"Gabe, I-I don't know where to begin."

Gabe didn't hesitate. "Look, Fiona, I really don't have time for this. Say what you gotta say or go."

"Okay, okay." I replied. "But, just promise you'll hear me out."

Gabe nodded as he looked at me. "Of course. Go ahead."

Reaching up, I crossed my hands at my chest. "Gabe I just want you to know how much I respect and admire what you're doing with the Link Protocol and with medicine, in general. I think you are a visionary and that the work we are doing here will positively impact the lives of millions of people."

Gabe waved me off. "Fiona, I'm not looking for an ego stroking here, okay? I appreciate it, but it's not necessary."

"I know that," I began. I inched forward in my seat, tilting my upper body towards him. "Just please, let me finish."

Gabe shook his head once or twice and leaned back in his chair. "No, Fiona. I don't have time right now. Look, there's a lot to do and not much time left. I'm frustrated with you right now, yes, but nothing more. Let's leave discussions about what's going on between us for a later time. All right?"

As soon as he finished speaking, I felt a strange mix of disappointment and relief. Disappointment in the fact that he'd stopped me before I could tell him how I felt, but at the same time, relief in the sense that my frustrations apparently hadn't damaged our relationship.

"Yes, okay." I said.

"Is there anything else right now, Fiona?"

I shook my head and prepared to get up from the chair. "No. Not right now."

"Okay then." Gabe said.

Reaching for the arms of the chair, I began to push myself into a standing position, when all of a sudden Gabe snapped his fingers.

"Oh!" he began, as he flipped through several pieces of paper on his desk. "I forgot to mention something about the clinical trial data that we've been getting back…"

"Oh, yes?" I replied.

Gabe licked his fingertips and gestured for me to wait as he continued to thumb through the stack of paper on his desk. I could tell from his expression that whatever the news was, it excited him.

"Well, now I'm intrigued." I said.

Without lifting his head, Gabe glanced up at me. "You should be... Oh, here we go."

After locating the information he'd been searching for, Gabe spent the next several minutes explaining that the trials had uncovered something remarkable... a possible novel usage for cancer treatment.

In essence, the treatment worked by robbing the cancer cells of what they need to thrive and multiply. For lack of a better term, the cancer cells would starve to death. This was all hypothetical, of course, but the possibility did exist. Even so, the clinical trials were in their early stages and so any experimental treatments were still a long way off.

Obviously, I thought about my grandmother. Surely someone with her advanced illness would be able to participate. However, unless by some miracle that came to pass in the next six months, it would be far too late for her.

About the only thing that would give her more time would be another round of chemotherapy. I hadn't anticipated this turn of events. But if there was any chance that the protocol could be adapted for possible treatment, it wouldn't matter if she wasn't around to receive it. Maybe this news would be the push she needed to go once again.

After Gabe finished telling me, a completely random thought popped into my head. Exciting though it was, it seemed odd he'd mentioned the news to me. Could he know about my grandmother somehow? I hadn't told Gabe anything about my personal life. What's more, he hadn't asked.

Even so, he had my curiosity piqued.

"Why are you telling me this, Gabe?"

"What do you mean? Why wouldn't I?"

"No, I mean the possible cancer treatment application. That's not information you needed to share."

"Of course it is, Fiona. You'd be the first one who ought to know. Especially in your situation."

I swallowed. "My situation?"

"Yes," Gabe said with a slow nod of his head. "You're the one giving the presentation, remember? If there's any possibility, however remote it might be, to discuss the Link Protocol in the framework of cancer treatment, you can bet your ass you'll be doing it."

"Of course," I replied, as I realized he didn't know about my grandmother after all. "Right."

"You can handle it, Fiona. Trust me, I'll brief you on it personally if need be."

He winked at me as he finished speaking.

"Oh, I see."

Gabe nodded and leaned back in his chair. The icy demeanor he'd displayed towards me minutes earlier before began to soften.

"Yes," he said with a smirk as he interlocked his fingers across his chest. "It's been a while since you've had a good briefing. And I know just the place to do it…"

I felt the hint of a smile curl in at the corner of my mouth. "I'm sure you do. May I inquire as to where that might be?"

"St. Barths," Gabe replied without hesitation. "Gorgeous fucking place… In the Caribbean. Ever been?"

"Gabe, you've seen where I live. What do you think?"

Gabe nodded and leaned forward in his chair. "You'll love it. You couldn't hope for a better place to have the presentation. All the investors will be there, relaxing and having a good time. Trust me, you'll float through the presentation."

"Oh, so the presentation is in… St. Barths?"

"Yes," he said with a nod. "Is that a problem?"

I shook my head and lied. "No."

So now, not only did I have to finalize all the lab work and nail down the highlights for the presentation, but I had to somehow arrange someone to care for my grandmother while I was gone.

Since the accident years ago, we'd never been apart. Not more than twenty-four hours in over a decade. I shuffled in my seat as uncertainty about what I'd tell her and how I'd make this happen flooded my thoughts.

"Everything all right, Fiona? I thought you'd be happy about getting to travel."

"What?" I said, still half-trapped in the myriad of decisions I'd have to make. "What did I say?"

"Well, you didn't say anything. You just seem uncomfortable about doing it."

"I don't get to travel much. I'm not crazy about flying."

"Well, you're not flying coach, honey. Trust me. You'll love it."

GABE

After Fiona left my office, I realized how nice it was to see a smile on her face again.

With any luck, giving her something like the trip to St. Barth's to look forward to might perk her spirits up. I felt as if I'd been even-handed and fair with Fiona since she came to work here. Even so, the banter we'd shared when we met had all but vanished in recent weeks.

I only caught glimpses of it now.

Gone was the shy but feisty woman I met at the bar that night. She hadn't been afraid to engage in a bit of back and forth with me then, but now it was as if she was shadow of her former self.

Something didn't add up. She had everything she could have wanted out of this situation, and more. She was making terrific money, doing work she loved, and putting her career on a trajectory most people her age would be thrilled to have.

But Fiona seemed distant, unhappy.

Had I caused that change in her somehow? I'd never been dishonest with her or misled her in any way about what was happening between us. But at some level, I couldn't help but feel responsible. I sat in my chair, propped my elbows on the arms, and tented my fingers together, considering where I'd gone wrong.

She played my revelation about the possible cancer treatment emerging from the clinical trials close to the vest. I didn't even get so much as a raised eyebrow from her. On the other hand, I had no idea how advanced her grandmother's illness was at this point. But not to have any reaction whatsoever seemed strange.

Just then, I stood and rounded my desk, and as I did, I passed by the chair Fiona sat in minutes earlier. I caught a passing whiff of her perfume as it lingered. I wasn't good with flowers and such, but the scent was something I'd expect to smell on a springtime stroll.

I continued across my office and walked towards the vast expanse of windows, which provided me views as far as I could see. I made my way into the bright yellow glow of the afternoon sun and stopped as the first streaks of warmth stretched across my face. Allowing my gaze to wander, I took in the horizon as I ruminated.

I wanted to understand Fiona's problem. Without doing so, getting her to deliver the presentation I needed would be difficult, if not impossible. The past few weeks, and especially the last couple of days, were evidence of that fact.

Now more than ever, I seriously considered confronting her with what I knew.

But would that cause her to pull further away or bring her closer to me? Where Fiona was concerned, I wasn't so certain any longer. I made lazy laps along the entire length of the windows as I considered the situation. Then another realization hit me.

I hadn't slept with anyone else since she came to work for me. Granted, I'd been swamped with work on the Link Protocol. Any time I was the midst of a massive project, my libido took a back seat. But… no, this was something different.

Since the first time I'd slept with her, I couldn't recall having interest in any other woman, whether in the office or outside it. I wasn't sure what that meant, but I wasn't so dim as to think it meant nothing at all either.

Perhaps at some level, I wanted to see where things would go with her. Well, more specifically, the Fiona I met at the bar. The new version of Fiona… I couldn't say the same thing.

Maybe I was being a bit too hard on her. After all, she wasn't missing a beat in the lab. As far as the presentation went, I still had confidence in her. Perhaps what she and I needed right now was to get back to the way things used to be a bit.

If I were to lighten things up, she'd relax.

Would it work? I had no idea, but it was far superior to continuing on the current path.

FIONA

Even though Gabe and I seemed to have patched things up for the moment, I'd never been under so much pressure in my life.

I still hadn't been sleeping well. But with the presentation on the horizon now, I had no choice but to focus more and more of my time on it. The sleep deprivation was starting to take a toll. During the hours I was awake, which was about twenty of them a day now, I yawned almost at an uncontrollable level.

It goes without saying I had trouble concentrating both on my own work and in meetings with the team. In the past few days, I'd begun to experience limited mobility in my neck. It got so bad for a day or so, I could barely turn it in one direction or the other.

Yet, knowing how important everything was and how much we all had on the line, I needed to do whatever I could. In no way did I want to let the team, Gabe, my grandmother or myself down. So if I had to push myself a little harder than normal, I would.

Most of what remained to be done was my responsibility, so even if I wanted to get help, I couldn't. Gabe was counting on me, and in the wake of our last conversation, I wanted to do whatever was necessary to make him proud he'd made the decision he did.

Yet as the days wore on, the fatigue continued to mount. At this point, I more or less lived on coffee and soda. And so it was I sat at my workstation, and as I looked down at the page, I began to see spots of light. Small at first, they grew in diameter, and before long, I found it difficult to make out my notes at all. I tried blinking my eyes and rubbing them for at least a minute straight, thinking they were perhaps just tired.

Yet, even with my eyelids closed tight, the blotchy bright spots remained. By now, there was no use trying to write, as I couldn't even see the page a foot from my face. I opened my eyes once more to try and adjust my vision, and it was around that time the room seemed brighter than normal. And not just a little brighter but much, *much* brighter, to the point where I felt the need to shield my eyes.

As if that wasn't enough, the slightest sound seemed deafening all of a sudden. I pressed the tips of my fingers against my ears, squeezing my eyes closed tight in the process. Hunched over my workstation, a sour taste entered my mouth, as I struggled against a sudden rush of nausea.

What the hell was happening to me?

It wasn't long before Andrew noticed my obvious discomfort and made his way towards me. I felt his fingertips touch my shoulder, but the force of it seemed magnified by the sheer fact it caused me to move.

Now rocking back and forth in my chair, I moaned, deep and long.

"Fiii-oo-nnn-aaa-hhh." His voice echoed inside my head like a thousand cymbals all crashing into one another at the same time.

"S-s-s-hh… s-s-s-hh…" I begged with a whisper, shaking in place.

Just then, I felt Andrew's hand press into the middle of my back. He began to rub it with small, gentle circles. Returning my hushed statement with a soft one of his own he said, "I think I know what's happening, Fiona. Can you stand?"

I remained motionless for a moment or so. After a shaky, shallow inhale, I cracked my eyelids a fraction and glanced towards Andrew. He stood above me with his hand extended. I reached for it and began to stand. As I did, I felt weakness come to my legs. Lurching for him, I grabbed hold of him just as I was about to fall. Even the small movement made it feel as if my head might split in two.

I whimpered as I clutched onto his shirt, burying my face in his chest.

"Come on Fiona," he said. "Hold on to me. We'll get you taken care of."

GABE

Believe it or not, it was the first time I'd ever been to the company infirmary. Not long after I made my way inside, an older woman who I assumed was the nurse approached.

"Mr. Hawkins?" she said, as she neared. "Sir... Are you ill?"

"What?" I replied, shaking my head. "No. I'm here about the woman you admitted not long ago, Fiona Matthews."

"Oh yes, Fiona. What about her?"

I looked past the nurse for a moment, surveying the entryway. It was as you might expect. An array of first aid equipment, a couple of exam tables and even a defibrillator. I didn't see Fiona anywhere. My perusal didn't go unnoticed.

"She's in there," the nurse said at last, as she gestured behind me.

I turned in place and looked down a short hallway, not more than about twenty feet in length.

"It looks like the lights are off in there," I said, as I did a half-turn back towards the nurse.

"Mmm, hmm. Yes."

"Why? What's wrong with her?"

Over the next several minutes, the nurse explained she suspected Fiona suffered from an acute migraine, most likely brought on by stress. For the better part of an hour, Fiona had been unable to move, much less speak. The nurse had only been able to talk to Fiona in the past fifteen minutes. It was the nurse's opinion that once she was able to get some of the things causing her stress under control, her symptoms should improve.

As she finished, I raised my hand to my chin and rubbed it, as I considered the fallout. If this handicapped Fiona to such an extent she couldn't function in the lab, let alone do the presentation in St. Barths, well, I needed a new plan and I needed it fast.

"I see," I said as my eyes met the nurse's. "And, if removing the stress doesn't help her to improve?"

The nurse glanced towards the room with Fiona in it before she replied. "Well understand, this isn't really my area of expertise, Mr. Hawkins. To get a definitive answer, you'd have to consult with a specialist. I'm not in a position to…"

"Yes, okay, I understand," I said with a casual wave, cutting her off mid-sentence. "Let me rephrase the question. If we're able to get her past this initial episode and remove some of the stress… If the headaches were to clear up, it would be reasonable to assume they were acute and not chronic. Would that be a fair assessment?"

The nurse considered my question for a moment or so.

"Yes," she said with a slow nod. "Of course, it's still possible this is the onset of a chronic condition. But we'll only know that for sure after the stressors have been removed, followed by a period of time to see if they return."

"Okay, well, I think that answers my question."

As I finished speaking, I gestured towards the dark examination room with a nod of my chin. "Is she asleep?"

"No. No sir, she hasn't been sleeping. I'm keeping the room dark as it reduces the impact of light on her condition."

"All right. Well, is it okay to go in and see her?"

The nurse answered in the affirmative but added I'd need to keep my visit as short as possible and keep my voice as close to a whisper as I could.

"Thank you," I said, as I turned and began to walk towards the exam room.

"Of course, Mr. Hawkins."

A few moments later, I eased the door to the room open. The hydraulic swing arm emitted a slow, persistent hiss. Cracking the door open just wide enough to fit inside, I walked through and closed it behind me as quickly as possible. Engulfed in near darkness, I turned towards the center of the room.

It took a moment for my vision to adjust, but when it did, I noticed the curves of Fiona's figure as she lay on an exam table in the middle of the room. I walked towards her with a heel to toe motion, pressing the soles of my feet hard into the flooring to keep the sound to a minimum. After a half dozen steps or so, I stood over Fiona. Keeping the nurse's admonition in mind about whispering, I started to speak with as soft a voice as I could.

"Fiona," I began. "Are you able to talk to me?"

She shifted her body a bit as I finished speaking.

Under ordinary circumstances, the sound of her crinkling the thin paper covering the exam table would have hardly caught my attention. In the still quiet, however, it was noticeable. Fortunately, though, Fiona didn't seem to be too bothered by it. With a slow roll, she turned her body in my direction. The harsh light of the hallway in the infirmary shone through a small window on the exam door. With her face half-concealed in shadow, Fiona looked at me through hazy blue eyes.

"I'm so sorry, Gabe. I-I don't know what happened."

"Well, according to the nurse, you experienced an acute migraine headache. She said it's caused by stress."

Fiona looked away from me. I sensed the regret she had over it. Even so, these things happened to people from time-to-time. Now wasn't the time to wallow in it. We'd have to confront whatever it was that put her here and deal with it.

And in that instant, the perfect solution came to mind.

"Fiona," I began, as I moved closer to her. "Look, I've got an idea. We're going to take a few days off. Just you and me. I've got a standing reservation at a suite in a hotel and spa not far from here, about an hour's drive. We'll spend a few days there and unwind. You'll be good as new, I promise."

As much as she could, Fiona rolled her head back and forth on the pillow in disagreement.

"Thank you for the offer but I can't afford to be gone from the lab, Gabe. Not right now."

After a soft chuckle, I leaned against the bed. With a tender stroke, I swept the back of my hand across her forehead. I hadn't been this close to her in a while and frankly, I missed it. There were any number of little things, of course, but mostly it was her voluptuous curves, perfectly kissable lips and the delicate fragrance of her perfume. As my fingers slid off her cheek, Fiona turned her head toward them, nuzzling her soft flesh against me.

"Fiona, I know what it's like to work as hard as you have been, all right? I built this place from nothing, with my wits, my balls and a dream. Of all the people you know, I'm the one who relates to what you're going through more than anyone else. And let me tell you, the body has a way of making choices the mind thinks are the wrong ones. Right now, what your body is telling you is that you need a break. There's still a lot of work ahead, and now is not the time to be in a situation like this."

"I know," she whispered. "I'm sorry. So very sorry."

"It's okay, Fiona."

She looked exhausted, utterly spent. In spite of her protests, I had the real sense she was on the verge of agreeing with me, so I moved in to close the deal.

"Look, this is *my* company and *my* investment. The simple fact is that I need you, Fiona. I need you healthy. I can reschedule things. There's still enough time. You need this and I'm not taking 'no' for an answer."

She hesitated for a moment. "Gabe, believe me, I would love to, but I've got some family responsibilities outside of the office. They can't be helped."

Of course she spoke about her grandmother. I decided to see if she'd make mention of it.

"Why can't they be helped? Do you have to be the one to do it?"

"What do you mean?"

"Can you hire someone? You know, to do whatever needs to be done while you come with me?"

"Of course I could, Gabe. But I can't afford it. Anyway, I-I'd rather not discuss it."

"No problem," I said with a nod. "I understand. How about this... I'll reimburse you for hiring someone. Just think of it as part of the vacation."

Shaking her head, Fiona began to speak. "No, Gabe, I can't, I..."

But no sooner had she started than she emitted a shaky moan. Wincing, Fiona slid her fingers into her hair and fell silent.

"This won't do, Fiona. Get your home situation handled or I'll do it for you. One way or another, you're coming with me."

She remained still for several moments until, without moving, she replied with a whisper, "Okay."

FIONA

As it was, I really had no alternative in the matter. When it was all said and done, it was Gabe's company.

So I did as he asked and found an in-home nurse to stay with my grandmother while we were away for a few days. I told her it was a mandatory work retreat Gabe wanted to hold to last-minute prep with the team. Whether she believed me or not, I wasn't certain, but she didn't press me either, so I assumed I'd more or less convinced her.

As far as Gabe was concerned, even though I appreciated the gesture, I committed to keeping my guard up while we were away. Instead, I wanted to do my best to keep things cordial. I didn't have the immediate sense that Gabe was taking me away for any other reason than what he told me, but I wasn't absolutely certain either.

On a positive note, my migraine symptoms relented the day before our getaway, giving me a bit of a respite and hopefully an opportunity to get rid of some of the stress I'd been dealing with.

We rode along in the back of limousine with the windows down. I looked out into the distance, and with my arm extended, I made waves with my fingers, curling them up and down over distant trees and knolls. As the miles streaked away beneath the tires, I closed my eyes and exhaled the first deep breath I'd had in months. It was wonderful to be away from the grind of the lab and the relentless pressure of the Link Protocol presentation.

It wasn't long afterward when Gabe spoke up to tell me about where we were going. I hadn't asked. Knowing Gabe, I was certain it would be fabulous. All I had to do was relax and take it easy for a few days. Rolling my head in his direction, I opened my eyes with a slow blink. Gabe sat less than a foot from me. The warm breeze filled the backseat, causing his hair to swirl around his face as he looked at me.

As my eyes locked on his, I realized the idea of keeping my resolve was to be much harder than I planned.

His tan jaw flexed, and as he began to tell me about the day's activities, my tongue slid from between my lips. Lucky for me the air was dry, otherwise I would have no explanation for the lip licking gesture.

"You'll love it, Fiona," Gabe said with a quick wink. He paused for a moment and reclined into his seat. "Especially what we're doing as soon as we arrive."

"Mmm, can't wait," I said, as I smiled and rolled my head away from him, closing my eyes once more. A myriad of activities flashed in my consciousness. Mani-pedi, mud bath, hot stone massage… The list of pleasurable activities swelled as rapidly as my desire to kiss Gabe had moments earlier.

"Great. Hopefully you've never done it before. I'd love to be your first."

Never done it before? Who hasn't had a mani-pedi or a massage? After all, what else was there to do at a luxury spa and hotel? I tilted my head up and swiveled it in his direction. With one eye opened, I muttered, "Done what?"

Gabe winked.

Two hours later, a swirl of dust and dirt came up from behind us as Gabe hit the brakes on a Jeep we'd picked up as soon we'd arrived, bringing us to stop with a semi-slide. I waved at the cloud as it passed by, doing my best to keep the particles from flying up my nose. As I did, Gabe jumped out of the driver's seat and headed around to the rear of the vehicle. In less than ten seconds he reappeared to my right, clutching a large knapsack.

"Come on," he said with a smirk. "We walk from here."

As grateful as I was to get away, so far this wasn't looking like the kind of trip I had in mind. Images of pampering began to fade from my consciousness.

Unable to control myself, I exhaled and grumbled. "Really? Do we have to?"

Gabe scoffed. "What? Are you nuts? Don't be ridiculous. Now come on. This will be worth it. Trust me."

Gabe began to walk away, and the sound of dry leaves and trail scrub crunched beneath his feet. I was not a backwoods kind of girl. As I climbed out of the car, I cursed at myself. I didn't want to come off as ungrateful, but at the same time, I was in no shape to hike for miles on end. Just then, I planted both feet on the ground and looked towards Gabe as he vanished into a thicket ahead. Looking up to the canopy above, I moaned and a moment later, I hurried after him.

After scampering down the trail, I turned in the direction Gabe had vanished in moments earlier, but he was nowhere in sight. I swallowed an anxious lump as I scanned the immediate area. After several moments, my voice crackled as I called out.

"Gabe! Where are you?"

Frozen in place, I thrust one hand down into the front pocket of my jeans. With my free hand, I reached down towards my charm bracelet and began to run my fingers over it. There was probably no reason for my concern, but it seemed as if I was alone all of a sudden.

Chewing my lip, I yelled once more. "Gabe! This isn't funny! Where are you?"

After a few more seconds of silence, Gabe finally replied. "Up here! Keep following the path. I'm at the top of the hill!"

It didn't take long, but it was an uphill walk, in a *small mountain* sort of way. At last, I arrived at the top, and as I did, I noticed Gabe there in the midst of preparing a picnic spread for us.

"Aww… a picnic?"

"Yep. Surprised?"

"Yes, of course."

Gabe chuckled as he pulled a blanket out from underneath his arm. Grabbing one end, he snapped the rectangular cloth in front of his face and then guided it down to the ground. I watched in disbelief as he picked up the knapsack, placed it in the middle of the blanket and began to unpack its contents.

"Did you do this, Gabe? All by yourself?"

"What?" Gabe replied as he glanced back over his shoulder. A bottle of Reisling appeared as he pulled his hand out of the knapsack. "You say that like you don't think I could put together a picnic."

"Well," I began, arching an eyebrow. "Did you?"

"Hmm, more or less," he said, as he continued to dig through the knapsack, producing plates, silverware and condiments.

"What does that mean?"

Pulling out sandwiches piled high with delectable roast beef, containers of fresh potato salad and even some apple pie for dessert, he continued. "Well, I told the hotel concierge about the idea for the picnic, and she put all of this together. Like I said, it was more or less my doing."

I chuckled and shook my head.

"Hey it's the thought that counts, right?" he said. "Come on, let's eat."

Smiling, I took a seat next to him as he prepared a plate for me. After he passed it to me, I bit into the sandwich. The salted roast beef, tinged with a bit of horseradish, melted in my mouth. I covered my lips with my napkin and muttered, "Oh my God, that is so delicious."

Gabe smiled as he tore a bite away from his sandwich as well. "Yeah."

Taking in the ideal weather and scrumptious food, we ate in silence for a few minutes. I took a sip of the Riesling after I finished speaking. Light bubbles of sweet apple and berry flavor slid down my throat. Across from me, Gabe wiped his fingers as he took a break and put his sandwich down on his plate.

"Beats a massage any day, doesn't it?"

I shook my head as I looked at him. "No."

Gabe leaned back, bracing himself with his arms. "Is that right? So you mean to tell me all this effort I went through isn't better than a massage. Is that what you're saying?"

I smiled at him as he chastised me.

"Well," I began. "First of all, you didn't put the lunch together, you told me the concierge did it. And secondly, you told me we were coming to this resort so I could be pampered and get rid of stress."

Gabe chuckled while I paused, but didn't say anything.

"And thirdly… Are you crazy? Of course I love it, Gabe. No one has ever done anything like this for me. Thank you. It's wonderful, and you're very sweet."

Gabe nodded as he leaned forward once more.

"That's more like it," he said with a wink.

I smiled, taking a sip of my wine as Gabe looked at me for moment.

"Hey," he said, as he patted the ground next to him. "Come on over."

GABE

Fiona set her glass down and stared at me.

"Gabe," she began with a stammer. "I um, I don't think I should."

"Why? Are you worried my wild side might be too much for you to handle out here in the wide open spaces?"

"No."

"Oh, I see. So you're worried you won't be able to control *your* wild side then. Is that it?"

"No, definitely not. I am in control."

I patted the ground once more. "Let's find out."

Fiona grimaced at me for a few seconds before at last giving in to my challenge. She stood and began to walk across the picnic blanket, but as she did, a bit of it bunched up under her foot and tripped her. Clutching her wine glass, Fiona shrieked as she started to tumble in my direction. I shot upright and grabbed hold of her, stopping her at the last instant and guiding her safely to the ground next to me.

"Wow, talk about throwing yourself at me. Some self-control…"

"Hah, hah, hah," she deadpanned through the beginnings of a frown.

As Fiona tried to gather her wits, I picked up her now empty wine glass and refilled it. Afterward, I passed the bubble-filled drink to her.

"You okay?"

Fiona took the glass from me. "Yes, thank you. I would have broken my neck if you hadn't caught me."

I leaned in towards her. "Yeah, probably. So… how are you gonna thank me for such heroic action?"

Fiona turned to look at me.

Midday sun shined down on us through the breeze-filled patchwork of leaves overhead. Looking into her eyes with an unflinching stare, I licked my lips. She took a quick sip of her wine, breaking her gaze. As she did, I reached up to her chin and slid a couple of my fingers beneath it. Curling them in my direction, I guided Fiona's face towards mine.

"Well?" I said.

"Well what?" she whispered.

"Have you figured out how you're going to thank me properly? You know from an almost certain death?"

Unblinking, Fiona sat motionless as I spoke to her. "No."

"I have an idea."

With that, I leaned in towards her. Fiona's body stiffened as I approached. I continued until I came within a couple inches of her lips, where I stopped. By then, the breeze had died down, and as I looked into Fiona's eyes the sound of her labored breath caught my attention.

Reaching up, I grabbed hold of Fiona's glass, took it from her and placed it on the ground. Afterward, I turned my attention back to her, noticing her eyes held a mix of uncertainty and anticipation. I slid my tongue from between my lips just enough to moisten them. Holding Fiona's gaze, I moved towards her mouth, and as I did, she took a deep breath.

But just before I reached her, I turned my head, moving it past her mouth and towards her neck. Reaching up, I slid my fingers behind Fiona's head, snaking them in her soft, blonde locks. The breath she'd held moments before escaped from her mouth as I pressed my lips against her exposed, milky flesh.

Fiona moaned as I began to kiss and lick the entire length of her neck, eventually working my way up towards her ear, where I nibbled at it with tender, gentle nips. As I did, Fiona tilted her head towards me, nuzzling her cheek to mine. With my hand still intertwined in the silky smoothness of her hair, I gently turned Fiona's face towards mine and crushed my mouth into hers.

A mix of a whimper and a groan emerged from Fiona as I slid my tongue inside her mouth. Hearing that sound from her stirred my already hard cock, stiffening it further. Her kiss tasted sweet and carried with it a hint of alcohol from the Riesling she'd drunk. It was a heady mix and one that had me hypnotized.

With my other hand, I reached down and grabbed hold of her at the waist, squeezing as I did. Fiona draped her arms across my shoulders, grasping them together behind my head with a loving embrace. For several moments we continued to kiss, out in the open under a warm afternoon sun and easy, gentle breeze until at last, she spoke.

"Gabe, it's not that I don't want to. I do. But…"

I just looked at her and shook my head without speaking a word. I rose to my knees and straddled her, helping Fiona to lie down on top of the picnic blanket. Looking into her eyes, it was plain to see that she was conflicted. But no matter, she remained silent, staring up at me in anticipation of what I'd do next.

So I obliged…

Reaching down, I slid my fingers inside her jeans, pinching the denim and snap between my fingertips. In less than a second, I'd unfastened them and begun to unzip them, when Fiona pushed herself up onto her elbows.

"Gabe…"

Ignoring her, I continued to remove her clothing.

In spite of her words, Fiona's body spoke its own language. As I tugged at the jeans, she lifted her hips off the ground, helping me to remove them much easier. After sliding them off her legs, I tossed them to the side and turned back towards her once again. Now, with only her panties remaining on her, I stood and began to undress.

If she was going to protest or beg me to stop, this would have been the time.

But Fiona said nothing as I removed my clothing, and before long I'd returned to the blanket once more, straddling her, wrapping my fingers around my hard dick. With my free hand, I reached towards her panties and hooked a finger inside them.

As before, Fiona put up no resistance and once again moved her hips in a way to assist. Now she was completely exposed before me. I positioned myself between her thighs one last time, spreading them as wide as they would go.

Fiona broke her gaze on me and instead looked down towards my cock.

With one hand at the base of my dick, I descended towards her until the tip touched the soft folds. I lingered there for a moment until our eyes met.

"Fuck me, Gabe," she whispered, giving in to her need. "Fuck me."

I nodded and without wasting another second, pushed myself inside her. Moaning, she lifted her legs, wrapping them around my backside. Fiona shivered and trembled beneath me as I claimed her.

As I leaned over, she hooked her arms around my torso, matching the grip she already had on me with her legs. I began to thrust inside her, slowly at first. It had been so long since I'd fucked her, I wanted to savor every possible moment. Her pussy was so wet and tight. The suction of it along the length of my cock sent a raging fire through me.

"Fuck…" I moaned, feeling as if I might cum at any instant.

Fiona looked up at me and licked her lips, inviting me to consume her once again. I lowered my head in response and covered her mouth with mine. With my tongue inside, I began to run it along the insides of her teeth, tasting her. All the while, I continue to drive myself deeper inside her with each stroke.

Soon, the only sounds I became aware of were Fiona's gentle moans of pleasure and the distinctive slap of skin on skin as my pelvis collided with her curves. With each stroke, I felt my balls crash into her as my dick hardened in readiness for what approached.

For several minutes I continued to thrust inside her, over and over, and with each successive pulse it seemed as if my cock grew harder, fuller, longer. Fiona looked up at me through eyes hazy with lust. Reaching towards my chest, she placed her palm flat against it and caressed the fine sheen of perspiration that had begun to show.

She dragged her fingers down the midline of my torso as I continued rock my hips back and forth. As she did, her nails curled under, digging into my flesh like a feral cat, until at last, she reached my midsection. After another stroke or two, Fiona shifted her hips to indicate she wanted to be on top.

I obliged, and after a quick readjustment, Fiona swung her leg over my torso and straddled me, grabbing hold of my cock with her small hand. With the other planted firmly on my chest, Fiona guided my rock hard dick towards her pussy.

Wasting no time, she slid on top of me, taking my entire length inside of her. I licked my lips as she descended. Once she'd gone as far she could, Fiona paused for a moment, stripped away her shirt and soon afterward her bra. She tossed them aside. As she did, I reached up towards her full, perfect tits, squeezing them. Fiona's head fell back, causing her to arch her ample breasts in my direction.

Under the midafternoon sun, Fiona's fair complexion shined. Releasing her tits from my grasp, I dragged my fingers down her hourglass torso until they reached her hips. With a firm squeeze, I got Fiona's attention once more. Her head tilted forward, and as if on command, she began to slide up and down on my cock.

Soon after, she leaned forward and pressed both palms hard into my chest. I swung my hands around, grabbing her ass. Fiona's head dipped further forward until her face disappeared behind her hair.

I watched her body bend and bow as she rode me. Fiona grunted and groaned each time she descended, until at last, the action of her hips began to increase in both speed and intensity. She stretched her torso forward, laying it flat against mine and tilting her ass up in the process.

Fiona wriggled her way up towards my lips and pressed her mouth against mine. By now, her hips slapped against me with a terrific crack each time she bounced up and down. She kissed me, humming into my mouth in a way that signaled the inevitable was upon her.

Releasing my hands from her ass, I drew them up into her hair, grabbing it into two fistfuls and pulling her mouth away from mine. Fiona gasped for breath, her lips puffy and swollen with desire. She nodded at me in silence, clearly indicating what was happening to her.

"Is it time? Are you ready?"

Fiona sucked in her lower lip biting it with her teeth. "Mmm, hmm..."

After a brief nod, I pulled her lips to mine once again, and as I did, Fiona cried out into my mouth. Her tongue lashed at me as orgasm overwhelmed her, causing her body to shake and tremble. As it did, she pumped her hips several more times in rapid succession until at last she slammed them hard into my pelvis, holding them there.

"Mmmm, mmm, mmm!!!!" she moaned into my mouth.

All the while, my hands remained in her hair, twisting and pulling at it as I consumed her. As her climax began to recede, once again I broke my lips free of hers, and with my hands on her shoulders, I guided her back into an upright position.

"My turn," I growled.

Fiona closed her eyes and licked her lips as I reached down and grabbed hold of her hips once more. Placing my feet flat on the ground I bent my legs at the knee. I lifted Fiona just a bit and began to thrust upwards. When I did, her entire body rippled with each powerful pulse of my cock.

I couldn't remember a time when my dick had ever been so hard.

"Fuck, fuck!" I yelled.

Unconsciously, I began to increase the speed, claiming her harder and faster with each stroke. I could feel it coming and I could hardly wait. Fiona rocked back and forth on top of me listing from side to side as I fucked her, ravishing her with violent thrusts on the exposed hillside.

And then, in a fraction of a second, my moment had arrived. With a single hard thrust, I claimed her with my entire length, causing her to emit a deep groan of pleasure. As she did, my cock pulsed inside her and I released my fire. I banged my head backwards, slamming it down to the ground as I emptied myself inside her. Arching my back, I squeezed Fiona's hips and came so hard I thought I might lose consciousness.

Yet as the seconds ticked by, I managed to avoid it, and soon after, I felt the rigidness from my orgasm begin to leave my body. Around that same time, Fiona tipped forward, falling into me with exhaustion. I dragged my fingertips up and down her backside, through her hair and towards her chin.

Tilting my head up off the ground, I drew my mouth towards hers. As our lips met, I tasted the salty hint of perspiration from her efforts. We kissed with gentle, soft smacks for a minute or so. The entire time I stroked her hair and savored the feel of her skin against mine as we relaxed in the aftermath.

It wasn't long after, about five minutes or so, when we'd started to get dressed.

As we did, I tried to make small talk with Fiona. Of course, I'd promised her a relaxing vacation and I still had every intention of fulfilling that commitment. I quizzed her about what she'd like to do first. I'd arranged for her to have any spa treatment she liked, whenever she would like it. She just had to let the concierge know.

Yet, as the minutes ticked by, I began to sense Fiona growing more distant. In fact, it wasn't long before she stopped answering me with sentences and eventually only grunts of acknowledgment.

After putting on my shirt, I looked at her and said, "Is everything okay?"

Fiona looked at me for only a moment before turning away. I wrinkled my brow.

"Hey. What's going on? Are you all right?"

Fiona didn't turn to look at me but instead only shook her head.

"Gabe, I'd like to go, please."

"Yeah, okay. We will. Let's clean up here and…"

"No," she said, interrupting me. "I mean, I want to go home. I don't want to be here."

My forehead tightened as confusion spread across my brow. "Huh? What the hell are you talking about, Fiona?"

By now, she'd stood up and was tugging on one piece of clothing after another in rapid succession. She didn't say a word until she'd finished, when she snapped her arms in front of her chest, crossing them and closing herself off to me.

In the meantime, I'd continued to pack up the remnants of our picnic. I paused as Fiona turned her back to me. She proceeded to walk several feet away, where she stood in silence for the next minute or so, as I finished collecting our things.

Once I had, I stood, brushed a bit of dust from my clothing, and walked in her direction. When I neared, I reached down to slip my hand around her waist but as I did, she pulled away.

"Okay, Fiona," I began. "I'll bite. You mind telling me exactly what the problem is?"

Yet, she didn't turn to face me. In a soft voice, more mutter than whisper, she replied, "It's nothing. I'd just like to go home. To my apartment."

"Just like that? I don't understand. Why?"

After dropping the knapsack on the ground, I leaned away from her and spread my arms wide. "Look at this place. Why would you want to leave? This is for you, Fiona. You can have anything you want."

She remained silent for a moment or so. "What I'd like… is to go home."

"Fiona," I said, as I reached for her. She tried to pull away once more, but I held firm and instead spun her back to face me. As I did, she looked up at me through glassy eyes.

"Gabe, please," she said. "Coming here with you was a mistake. I-I never should have done it. I'm sorry. Will you please... just take me home?"

I shook my head in disbelief.

"What's gotten into you, Fiona?"

While I spoke, Fiona reached up and smeared tears away from her cheek. I moved to try and console her, but she stepped away, increasing the distance between us.

"Fiona. Are you... afraid of me?"

She shook her head as I spoke. "No, Gabe. I'm not. That's not what this is about. I promise. It's just me, okay? It's me."

I drew my lips inward, pinching them tight against one another. After what just happened between us, this was the last thing I expected.

"Fiona, this is not gonna work."

She nodded, looking down at the ground. "Okay."

"What do you mean 'okay'?"

"I mean okay. If you say it's not going to work, I'm not going to argue with you, Gabe."

"So, no more of... *this*? That's fine with you?"

Fiona blinked in rapid succession as the tears began to flow with greater frequency. "I-I can't do this, Gabe. I-I can't."

"Do what? Fiona, I still have no idea what you're talking about. But hey, you know what? If that's the way you want it, no problem with me."

No sooner had the words left my lips than Fiona began to sob uncontrollably.

I looked at her. There was a part of me that wanted to console her, because I really didn't think this was all my fault. But then there was another part of me that wasn't real fond of being insulted. That was especially true in light of everything I'd done for her up until now, including this trip. Instead, I threw the knapsack across my shoulder and walked right past Fiona. I hadn't gotten more than five feet from her when she called out.

"Gabe! Where are you going?"

I continued on, my steps unbroken and my pace unchanged.

"To the car, Fiona," I grunted. "You said you wanted to leave. Go home. Remember?"

Just then, I heard a rapid succession of footsteps close from behind. The bottoms of Fiona's shoes skidded with jagged fits and stops along the dusty trail.

"Gabe, I-I'm so sorry. Please don't be angry."

"Too late."

"I knew coming here was a mistake," she began. "I-I knew it…"

As Fiona's voice trailed off, I stopped cold and spun in place. She'd been so close behind, the abruptness caught her off guard and she bumped into me. Startled, Fiona backed away a step or two.

"You know something, Fiona?" I said, as I scowled at her. "You're right. It was a mistake. A huge fucking mistake. And you know who made it? I did. Me, Fiona. Do you wanna know why that is?"

Fiona's eyes widened. I watched as a hard swallow crept down her throat. Her face wrinkled with concern while she bit her lip.

"No. I don't," she replied, as she shook her head.

"Simply, it's because I was wrong about you, Fiona. I hate to admit it, but in this case, I was wrong."

She looked at me in silence for a moment. As she did, a breeze passed between us, disturbing her hair. She reached up and cleared it free from her eyes as she spoke.

"What… What do you mean?" she stammered. "I thought you liked my work."

"This isn't about your *work*, Fiona. You're a fine scientist and you're turning into a great leader. No, this is about *Fiona the Woman*. That's what I was wrong about."

Fiona looked away from me and sniffled for a few moments. It took everything I had inside not to leave her on the hillside. I shook my head in utter disgust.

"Maybe you should quit, Fiona. Spare yourself from the misery of being with me. Please, nothing would make me fucking happier right now. Because this shitty attitude of yours needs to change. You need to appreciate who I am and what I do for you, okay?"

Fiona balled her fists in protest. "I never said I don't!"

"Well, what the hell am I supposed to think right now, Fiona? For someone who's so appreciative, you've got a funny way of showing it."

Fiona's angelic face turned sinister as she barked her response. "Go to hell, Gabe!"

I stepped toward her, hovering the tip of my index finger less than an inch from her chest. "You ever say something to me like that again, I'll fire you. You got me?"

"Well, if you do… I-I'll sue you for sexual harassment."

I couldn't believe what I was hearing. Something had gotten into her. What it was I had no idea, but I also had no intention of standing underneath a blazing hot sun while she made nonsensical threats towards me. I shook my head and made the last statement I would on the matter.

"You're welcome to try, Fiona. God knows it's happened plenty of times. With zero percent success rate, so you know."

Fiona scowled at me as I paused.

"You women, man, you're all the goddamn same. It's like you have this innate desire to fuck a good thing up. You know, self-sabotage. Tell you what, I'll save you the trouble. Now let's go get in the car and go."

GABE

The way Fiona and I left things... It didn't sit well with me.

The truth was that neither of us meant what we said on the hilltop at the resort.

She was pissed, and as much as I hated to admit it, I was reacting to it.

I should have handled the situation differently. It was less about the age difference between us than just knowing that sometimes in life, it's better to push back from situations when they get too emotional.

Fiona had her mind made up she wanted to leave the resort, probably before we even arrived there. I'd been around the block enough to see the warning signs. I missed them here. That's all there was to it.

I reached for my phone and dialed Holly.

"Yes, Gabe?"

"Holly my dear, get Fiona up here right away."

"Yes."

I placed the phone down in the cradle.

Getting up from my desk, I walked across my office to the well-stocked bar. I kept it for late night negotiations and the like, rarely using it myself. But with the day nearly over and my neck killing me from another sixteen hours of poring over briefs and data, I could use a stiff one.

After grabbing a rocks glass, I reached for the gin, followed soon after by a bottle of tonic water. Lining them up on the bar, I cracked the plastic top of the tonic water open. The hiss of carbonation filled the air as I placed it on the bar in front of me. As it settled, I reached towards the ice maker. Flipping it open, I scooped out enough for half my glass. A few seconds later, I'd added the gin and topped it with the tonic water.

I swirled it in the glass as I walked back across my office. The cubes *tinked* against one another and into the side of the glass. As I moved towards my desk, there was a knock at my office door.

"Come in."

As the door swung open, Fiona appeared. After turning and closing the door behind her, she began to walk towards me.

"You know what, Fiona?" I said, as she approached. "Have a seat at the conference table."

Fiona glanced at me for a moment and nodded her head. I noticed that as she took a seat, her old habit of clutching her sleeves inside her hands had made a return. Carrying my cocktail, I drew near the table and took a sip.

"Would you like something, Fiona?"

She shook her head. "No. No thank you."

"Suit yourself."

I pulled out the chair next to her and as I took a seat, I placed my beverage down on the conference table. With my hand wrapped around the ice cold glass, I looked at Fiona in silence for a moment. She returned my gaze and offered me a polite smile.

"Fiona, the reason I've asked you to come to my office has nothing to do with the work you're doing in the lab or with the presentation."

"No, I figured that."

"All right, well, do you know why I have asked you here?"

"Yes, I think so," she began. "Is it because of what happened at the resort?"

"It is, in part. But I think what happened at the resort is a symptom of some underlying issue between us."

Fiona swallowed hard as I finished my thought. I paused and lifted my cocktail to my lips, taking another healthy swig. After placing it back down on the table, I continued.

"You see, Fiona, I'm having difficulty understanding what the problem is."

Fiona straightened her arms beneath the table, closing herself off from me a bit.

"Like right now… Can you tell me why you feel the need to do that?"

Fiona exhaled a listless breath, and her shoulders slumped a bit. I watched her as she sat with her thoughts.

"Gabe, I've not done a good job of explaining my behavior toward you and that goes doubly true for what happened at the resort."

I nodded and took another sip of my drink as she continued.

"I've just been confused lately, and the last thing I want to do is risk losing my job."

"Your job is not at risk Fiona," I began. Placing my hand on the arm of the chair I straightened myself up into an upright posture. "What I'm talking about here has nothing to do with your performance at work. I believe I've told you that more than once already. Frankly, I don't understand why you don't believe me."

Fiona nodded and looked away from me. "I know. I don't know why I don't believe you either. I'm very sorry for that."

I leaned back in my chair and draped my elbow over the back of it. "Fiona, is there something else going on? Something else in your life that you want to tell me about?"

"What do you mean?"

"Well, let me ask you this another way," I began. "Do you enjoy spending time with me?"

A hint of a smile came to Fiona's mouth. I hadn't expected it. She nodded and replied, "Yes, I do. Very much."

"Okay, so if you were in my position, wouldn't you naturally assume that there is some other problem?"

"Of course I have problems in my life, Gabe. I just don't feel comfortable putting my personal issues out for the world to see, including you."

I nodded as I looked at her in silence for a moment. "Do you think that's fair to me?"

"I don't know. No, I guess. But that's just the way I am. I can't help it. I'm sorry. I don't expect you to understand."

"I get it Fiona. I'm a private person myself, so I understand where you're coming from. But here's what I don't do… I don't take out my frustrations on other people. And that's what I think you are doing here."

Without hesitation, Fiona shook her head and looked at me. "Gabe… That's not it. It's just…"

I waved her off in the middle of her reply. "Fiona, I really don't have a problem ending things between us. What I do have a problem with is you not being straight with me. As I've said before, you are under no obligation to sleep with me. I won't hold it over your head, and I won't allow it to affect anything relating to your work. Is that clear enough for you?"

She nodded. "Yes."

"All right then. Getting back to what happened at the resort… My intention was for you to enjoy yourself and get rid of the stress."

Fiona tugged a strand of hair behind her ear as she looked at me. "The picnic was nice."

I smiled and nodded. "Well, at least there was that, right?"

"Yes."

"But I did make a promise to you and I intend to make it right."

Fiona shook her head. "Gabe, please, it's not necessary. Everything is okay, really."

"Not to me it isn't Fiona. Look, I'm not expecting you to do or say anything in this situation, but we've got to do something to make this better for both of us right now, for the sake of the company."

"I promise, Gabe. You don't have to worry about it."

Ignoring her, I got down to the reason I'd asked her to my office in the first place. "Tell you what. Let's have dinner."

Fiona didn't hesitate. Shaking her head, she replied, "No, Gabe. I really don't think that's a good idea."

I waved her off as she protested.

"It's strictly business, Fiona. You and I still have a lot of work to do. The presentation is coming up fast now. Since that's the case, I'm going to have to insist."

Defeated, Fiona dropped her head a bit.

"Okay," she said with reluctance.

FIONA

I waited for Gabe outside the restaurant where I'd had my jealousy meltdown.

Between work and going home to take care of my grandmother, I had no time to shower and barely enough time to change. But so intense was my disdain for Mandy, the Uber Hostess, that I would rather sit on a bench across from the parking lot than deal with that slinky tower of sex.

Just then, Gabe's limo pulled up, and I stood and smoothed my dress. Squinting into the setting sun, I reached up and shaded my eyes with my hand as Gabe emerged from the rear of the vehicle.

"Hey," Gabe began, as he nodded in the direction of the entrance to the restaurant. "Why aren't you in the restaurant? It's hot as hell out here."

"Oh, I just got here," I lied.

Gabe stopped and leaned away from me. "But you're sweating and…"

But before he continued his thought, thank God, Gabe waved his hand with a casual flick.

"You know what. It doesn't matter. Let's just go."

Of course it would turn out she wasn't even at the hostess station as we entered. In fact, we passed right by it and continued straight through the restaurant. Gabe strode through as if he owned the place and walked right to his reserved table. As was the case with the last time I ate here, I looked up to several dozen pairs of eyes locked on me, as I slid into the booth.

What? Am I not good enough for him?

I was really beginning to hate this place.

I'd almost forgotten how much, in fact, until a nearly six foot tall living statue composed of tits and legs walked in our direction. As she arrived at the table, her gaze never wavered from Gabe and within a second, she leaned in, kissing him on the cheek.

Again!

I did my best not to stare but I couldn't help it.

I really, really, *really* was starting to hate this place.

She stood and looked at me, as if she hadn't noticed I was there when she walked up.

Please.

"Oh, hello again," she said.

I nodded in her direction, and as much as I wanted not to, I offered her a polite smile in return, but no words to accompany it. As luck would have it, it didn't matter much anyway. Her shift was just getting underway, so I hoped it was the last time I'd have to see her again.

Gabe was either oblivious or didn't care, because as I stared her down, he'd ordered a bottle of wine. Before long, the waiter returned and after uncorking it, he filled both of our glasses. Gabe reached down and slid the tips of his fingers around the stem. Nodding, he gestured for me to touch my glass to his.

As I did, he smiled.

"I'm glad you're here tonight, Fiona."

"Thank you."

When I tilted the glass to my lips, the scent of fruity alcohol hit me. I took a large gulp, more than I normally did, which I followed with another right away. I set my glass down and glanced towards Gabe. He hadn't noticed, as he'd been distracted searching for something in his suit coat pockets. As we locked eyes, he'd found what he was looking for, but he kept whatever it was concealed as he dropped it into his lap.

I ignored it for the moment as Gabe leaned back into the booth and in one smooth motion, flung his arm over the back of it. I offered him a polite smile, but not much more. I still wasn't even sure why I'd agreed to come here. We could just as easily discuss the presentation in the office, if that's why we were really even here. I had my suspicions.

Gabe didn't say a word, but instead moved an arm towards his lap. A moment or so later, it reappeared, and in his hand, Gabe held a jewelry box, which he placed in the center of the table. He set it down, but as he released it, he kept a single finger pressed to the lid of the box and looked at me.

"What is that?" I said.

Gabe flicked at the top of the box, nudging it a half-inch closer to me from where he'd placed it moments earlier.

"Open it."

I narrowed my gaze at him. Gabe smirked in return and nodded towards the small box.

"Hmm," I muttered, as I reached towards it.

Wrapping my fingers around the box, I picked it up and turned it in my direction. I had to admit to a sudden case of butterflies. I'd never been given a present by a man before, and knowing Gabe, it could be anything. Just then, I cracked the lid open and they appeared before me. I raised my hand to my mouth, covering it as I stared down at them.

"Gabe…" I whispered. "They're beautiful."

"Try 'em on."

Transfixed by their brilliance, I only half-listened to him. "But I don't understand… why?"

Gabe finished another sip of his wine. "Well, you know, for the way I behaved at the resort."

I glanced down at the diamond and jade encrusted earrings. Surely, Gabe would have saved what looked like tens of thousands of dollars in jewelry by just *telling me* he was sorry. They were beautiful though, more spectacular than anything I'd ever seen except behind glass at the jewelry store.

Of course, there was no way in *hell* I could accept them. Fortunately, I wouldn't have to turn him down based on his motives but my own small problem with ninety percent of all jewelry.

"They're exquisite, Gabe…" I paused, looking at them for emphasis.

"I sense a 'but' coming, Fiona."

"Well, it's just… Are they platinum?"

Gabe frowned and leaned away with a look of frustration on his face.

"What?" he scoffed.

"No, oh no…" I said as I leaned towards him. Draping my hand across my chest, I continued, "It's just that I'm allergic to everything but platinum. See?"

As I finished, I raised the arm where I wore my bracelet. Gabe's look of frustration melted into pure disgust as he exhaled.

"What? Gabe, I can't help it. It's not my fault I'm allergic."

He looked away from nodding and waving me off with a few casual flicks of his hand. "Yeah, yeah, okay, okay…"

Not even sure what I'd done wrong, I slumped into my chair a bit and turned my head away from Gabe and out into the restaurant, looking at nothing in particular.

Why hadn't I put a stop to this yet? What the hell was I doing?

It'd been weeks since I'd promised my grandmother I would, and yet here I sat, still unable to do it. But, I had to do it now, before things either got worse between us, or I reached a point where I couldn't turn back any longer.

"Gabe," I blurted out, before I hesitated for too long and lost my nerve. "I just can't do it anymore."

Lips pursed, Gabe rotated his head towards me with an unhurried swivel.

"Do what, Fiona?"

"I can't sleep with you anymore, Gabe. I can't. And as beautiful these are, I can't, I-I can't accept them."

With that, I stood and placed the jewelry box on the table in front of him. "I'm sorry, Gabe. I'm so very, very sorry."

Without giving him a moment to answer, I turned. With my head down and clutching my purse strap for dear life, I began to exit the restaurant.

"Fiona?" Gabe began, as I took my first couple of steps. "What the hell are you doing? We've got business to discuss."

I turned back towards him. By now, several pairs of curious eyeballs glued themselves to our discussion.

"Gabe, I can't. Please. I'm leaving."

I looked down at him, and his blue eyes sparkled with defiance. For another second, maybe two, we looked at one another, until at last, he nodded. Spinning the jewelry box in place as he stared at me, Gabe spoke.

"All right, Fiona. Go ahead."

I turned and left.

GABE

"Holly, get in here." I said, as I held down the intercom button on my phone.

The door to my office was open and it wasn't long before Holly rapped against it.

"Yes?" she said, as she peeked her head around the corner.

I looked up from my desk. Tapping my pen on the top of a stack paper with a series of quick strikes, I snapped, "Where's the updated prospectus?"

Holly took a few steps inside the office and closed the door behind her. Afterward, without a word, she marched towards my desk and stopped about a foot away, crossing her arms at her chest.

"It's right there," she said in a stern tone.

"Where? Because unless I'm *fucking blind*, I don't see it."

Unfolding one of her crossed arms, she aimed her index finger to a separate pile across from the one I'd rapped against moments earlier. "There, Gabe. Where I told you it was an *hour* ago."

I followed the line created by her stiff digit and reached for the white stack. I pressed the tips of my fingers on it and spun the pile of documents my direction.

"Well, why the hell are they here?"

"Gabe!" Holly exclaimed, as she stomped her foot.

"What Holly? What?" I barked.

"Stop it. Stop it right now! You have been acting completely ridiculous in the past few days and believe me, *everyone* has been noticing."

I scoffed and leaned back in the chair, tossing my pen on my desk. I interlocked my fingers and dropped my hands to my lap.

"Holly," I sputtered. "What the hell are you talking about?"

"Oh come on Gabe, you know exactly what I'm talking about!"

I raised my arms and slapped them down on the arms of my chair.

"Holly, look—I don't have time for any of this. Tell me what you're talking about or get the hell out of my office."

"I might. And not ever come back!" she said, as she bent from the waist, scowling at me.

I exhaled a shallow breath and reclined in my seat. "Go on."

In less than five minutes she proceeded to tell me that since I'd returned from my ill-fated spa retreat, I'd been short and grouchy with her. That got even worse after Fiona informed me at dinner the other night she wanted to end our arrangement. Of course, Holly didn't know about any of that.

"Holly, why are you being so sensitive? You don't get upset like this. I've been grouchy or whatever in the past. So what?"

"Mmm, hmm," she muttered, crossing her arms once more. For a moment, silence hung between us, until I heard the distinctive *pat, pat, pat* of her foot on the carpet in my office.

She unfurled her arms. They collided with the outsides of her thighs with a smack. "You're really going to make me say this, aren't you, Gabe?"

"Holly! Jesus! Say what?"

"Fiona. Fiona… Gabe."

"Fiona?" I replied. My brow tightened in a baffled frown. "Holly, I swear. If you don't tell me what the…"

Holly snapped her hands towards her face, cupping them around her mouth as she bellowed, "You have been sleeping with Fiona, Gabe! Something has happened between the two of you, and it's driving everyone crazy! Fix it!"

I blinked and looked at her in stunned silence.

Holly just shook her head. "Gabe, everyone knows it. This is something you've got to fix and fix fast. The way you've been acting… It won't be long before you have groups of people leaving at once. En masse…"

I really didn't know what to say. The idea of everyone knowing something was happening between Fiona and me didn't bother me. No. What bothered me was the fact I'd let the fallout from it affect not only my immediate future, but perhaps the future of Hawkins Biotech. The strangest part was, I'd been unaware of how I'd behaved.

"I'm being serious here, Gabe. With everything going on, you can't afford to act like this. I wouldn't be in here telling you this if I didn't respect you and everything you've done, okay? Just please, fix the situation, so you can get back to normal."

I raised my hand at her as she plead her case. "Okay, Holly. I understand. Message received. *Zero* distortion."

Her half-open mouth snapped shut. As it did, I nodded and pointed past her in the direction of my office door.

"Get Fiona. Tell her to come to my office. Bring her yourself if you have to. Got me?"

"Yes, Gabe," she said, as the first hint of a smile came to her face. "Gabe, can I just say that I…"

"No, Holly. You don't need to say anything. I'm responsible for this. Now, please do as I ask, and bring Fiona."

"Okay," she said with snap of her head in the affirmative. "I will."

After Holly left my office, I sat in my chair and reflected on what she'd said. In a way, I'd been guilty of the *very same thing* I told Fiona not to do. In other words, I was taking out my frustrations on other people at a time when I could least afford it.

In that instant, it became clear to me that the only way to fix this problem was to give it one more try with Fiona. I'd allowed her the leeway to decide whether or not she wanted to continue our arrangement. But as I reflected on my motivations, it seemed to me they were misplaced.

I wasn't about to let Fiona just end what was happening between us.

At the same time, I had to convince her to get past whatever was holding her back. If there was ever a time to be in salesman mode, this was it. Just then, in my peripheral vision, I noticed a figure appear in the threshold of my office. I looked up to see Fiona standing there, and for once, her hands weren't concealed in the sleeves of her shirt.

We looked at one another in silence for a moment and then I nodded at her.

"Come have a seat, Fiona."

I never got used to watching Fiona walk. For someone so uncomfortable with herself, she did move with feminine grace. I admired it as she approached, wanting nothing more than to have my way with her again. Of course, if that was to happen, I had a lot of negotiating to do.

I leaned back a fraction as she took a seat. "How are you?"

"Fine."

I've been around enough women to know that when they tell you everything is 'fine', it really means things couldn't possibly be any shittier and they are likely to get much, much worse.

"Good to hear," I said.

As I finished speaking, I turned my seat in her direction, facing her completely.

"Fiona, I'll keep this brief. The reason I've summoned you here is because the time is nearly upon us to leave for St. Barth's. I trust you will be able to make sufficient arrangements with your home situation."

Fiona nodded. "Yes, I'll use the same service I used when we went to the resort. It shouldn't be a problem."

"Very good. There is going to be one slight change to the schedule, however."

"Okay?"

"Yes. You and I will be leaving about a week ahead of time."

Fiona leaned away, pressing her back into the chair. With a tone of suspicion in her voice, she asked, "All right. Do you mind if I ask why?"

I nodded and leaned forward, interlocking my hands and placing them on the desk in front of me. "Because I said so. The simple fact, Fiona, is that I want to work with you on the presentation away from the distractions here at the office."

In obvious discomfort, Fiona shuffled in her seat. "Well, there's still a good deal of work to do as it relates to the clinical trials."

"That's true," I said, as I nodded. "But, all of those things can be easily delegated to Amanda and Melissa. Your role is much bigger than that, Fiona, and the time has come for you to step up and assume it. Of course, I'm not going to let you go through that alone. That's the reason you and I are going to be going to St. Barth's ahead of schedule."

Fiona swallowed hard. For several moments she sat in silence as I looked at her.

"You want to talk about it?"

"I just… I'm just not sure that the presentation is ready, that *I'm* ready."

Resting my elbows on the desk, I brought my hands together and started to rub them back and forth with an easy slide.

"That's understandable, Fiona. In fact, if you'd said anything else, I would've been concerned. But the simple fact is that we've got terrific science behind us, the research is solid, and we have more than enough to show the investors. You'll just have to trust me."

Fiona lowered her head and brought her hands together, looking at her fingernails.

"I do, Gabe."

FIONA

Prior to my meeting with Gabe, I'd been honing the presentation in the past week or so. My confidence ebbed and flowed, and it so happened when Gabe summoned me for the most recent discussion, I suffered from a good bit of doubt.

As far as Gabe's demand I go to St. Barth's ahead of time with him, I had mixed feelings. On the one hand, I was relieved Gabe was willing to help me polish the presentation. I was more than certain I'd see dramatic improvement with his help.

On the other, well, it meant I'd be alone with Gabe.

He'd been pleasant during our discussion. He didn't appear to be upset in the least with what I'd said to him at the restaurant. Knowing him though, I'd have to keep my guard up, since there was as good a chance as any he'd try something. But I really had no choice in the matter, so I resolved to be on guard and make the best of it.

With respect to the presentation, my hard work began to pay off. I'd grown much more at home speaking in front of crowds, thanks to my Toastmasters speeches. In addition, my position at Hawkins Biotech required regular meetings with the staff, during which I had to lead from the front of the conference room.

And, as if that weren't enough, I rehearsed in front of my grandmother on a regular basis. By now, she knew the speech as well as I did, and I wouldn't have put it past her to be able to deliver it in a pinch.

It so happened tonight was one of those nights, and as I wrapped up another dry run in her bedroom after dinner, we discussed where I could improve and shore up my weaknesses. The good news was that, little by little, my confidence grew.

And although my grandmother knew all about the presentation, she had no idea it was in St. Barths. I'd have to break the news to her sooner or later, and as we wrapped up my rehearsals for the night, the time had arrived.

I took a sip of a nearby glass of water with a bit of honey and lemon. It was supposed to work wonders on the throat when you're doing a lot of speaking. It must have worked to some degree, because since trying it, I hadn't had any issues. After two large gulps, I set the glass down on my grandmother's nightstand. The tart and sweet of the liquid swirled down my throat like a liquid candy cane. After I finished, I plopped down on the mattress next to my grandmother. The springs in the bedding squeaked as I settled at her side.

"Grandmother," I began. "We have to talk about a couple of things, all right?"

My grandmother reclined her head into her pillow. Rolling it towards me, she glanced up at me over the tops of her bifocals. Weary lines swept out from beneath her spectacles and deepened as she offered me a tired smile in response.

"Okay, dear. Is it about your presentation?"

"Yes. Well, yes and no."

"What do you mean?"

I cleared my throat, and after sliding a chunky strand of hair behind my ear, I began.

"Well, so you know I'm doing the presentation, but what you don't know is that I'm not doing it here… in town I mean."

"Oh," she said, as she paused and eased further back into the pillows. "Well, where will you be going?"

I spent the next few minutes explaining where St. Barths was and why Gabe felt it necessary to gather key employees and especially investors there. By setting up a casual meeting environment, he intended to have the whole process run a lot smoother.

My grandmother nodded as I spoke.

"Very good, dear. I'm so thrilled things are going well."

I reached down and wrapped my fingers around her forearm. With a curl of my digits, I squeezed the paper thin, near-translucent skin and frail muscles.

"Well, so I'll be gone for a while, Grandmother. You understand that, don't you?"

"Well, of course, Fiona."

"And you're okay with it?"

"What choice do I have Fiona? Even if I didn't want it, we need the money and your job is the only thing bringing it in for us."

"Okay," I said, as I smiled and released her arm from my grasp. "You know I worry."

"Don't, dear."

I explained to her I'd arranged for the same in-home nursing care I'd hired for my short-lived spa retreat with Gabe. She seemed more agreeable than I suspected. In the end, I assumed she probably realized there was no alternative. She was in no condition to travel, and even if she could, the meeting in St. Barths was far from a family outing.

"Honestly, Fiona," she said, as her eyes drifted closed. "You don't have a thing to worry about."

I chuckled. "You know that's not possible, don't you? I worry about everything."

"Yes, I do my dear. Try not to worry about this, though. I can assure you I'll be fine. I've got a bit of time yet before this cancer takes me."

I pursed my lips at her. "You know I hate it when you say things like that."

"I know, Fiona," she muttered.

I sensed sleep descend on her as she closed her eyes. If I didn't hurry, I wouldn't be able to tell her the other half of my story. Still relieved she'd reacted well to being left here with a nurse, I continued on to the more exciting part of the news, for her anyway.

"Listen, Grandmother. There's something else I need to tell you."

"I'm sorry my dear, but can it wait? I'm very tired."

I shook my head and reached towards her thigh, squeezing it a bit.

"No. It can't."

After another moment or so, my grandmother opened her eyes and nodded. "All right."

I'd debated telling her about the possible cancer treatment coming out of the clinical trials. The truth was that even if she could be accepted on an experimental basis, it was still a long way off. However, I reasoned that if I at least told her about it, perhaps it would give her the motivation she needed to seek chemotherapy. If she could hold on for a little longer, there was a chance she might live long enough to become a candidate.

And so, after a deep breath, that's exactly what I did. I told her everything I knew and what it would all mean to her.

She listened intently for several minutes until after a final nod, she looked at me and spoke.

"Well, so what's the difference between this treatment and everything else out there?"

"Good question, Grandmother," I replied. "It's a long explanation, but basically the treatment starves the cancer cells of the nutrients they need to survive and thrive. The best news of all is that it should pose no toxicity risk."

"So, it's not harmful to me, like the chemo?"

"It shouldn't be. No."

"I see."

Reminding her, I continued, "But the thing is, we're still a long way off from experimental trials, Grandmother. Even though you'd have an excellent chance to be a candidate, you still have to do chemotherapy to have any hope of living long enough."

No sooner had I finished than she shook her head and dismissed my suggestion with a wave of her hand.

"That's not living, Fiona. It's a living death."

I scooted closer to her. Taking her fingers in mine, I rubbed the back of her bony hand. "Grandmother, please. Just promise you'll think about it."

She looked at me without a word for a few seconds, until at last, she nodded.

"Okay dear, I'll think about it. I promise."

GABE

I loved being in St. Barths. Of course, I loved being in the office as well, but every so often it's nice to get away for a bit. While this wasn't just any ordinary getaway, a change of scenery was never a bad thing. The stakes were high for Fiona and frankly, even higher for me. To achieve the goals

I'd set for her presentation and for our arrangement, I'd need to have her as relaxed as possible.

And so it was after breakfast on our first full day on the island, I stood out on a large veranda connected to the dining room overlooking a nearby bay. I'd gotten up before Fiona and already had my breakfast. I stood at the edge, leaning my hip against the hardness of the wood railing. I looked out over the blue water, already dotted with a handful of sailboats and a few local fisherman returning from their early morning catch.

Drawing my gaze upward, I noticed a handful of seagulls high above the shore. They circled, dove and climbed, harnessing the power of the updrafts from the ocean to levitate themselves like tiny kites. Distracted by the serenity of it all, I hadn't heard her approach.

"Good morning," Fiona said, as she came to a stop a few feet behind me.

The sun wasn't yet up over the island's eastern-most cliffs, so I had no need to shield my eyes from it. Instead, as I turned to look at Fiona, it was as if in some ways I saw her again for the first time. Warm orange streaks and soft pink hues draped across her milky-white complexion like watercolors over a blank canvas.

To my pleasure and surprise, she looked at ease and rested. Not only that, but she was clad in a fine white hotel bathrobe that hugged her curves in all the right spots. I began to admire other assets besides her baby blue eyes and kissable mouth. My cock twitched. The silent, lust-filled stares didn't go unnoticed for long.

"Why are you looking at me like that, Gabe?"

I set my coffee cup on the railing.

"Just admiring the scenery."

Fiona rolled her eyes and shook her head.

Perfect. Nothing like getting under her skin a bit to start the day out right.

I winked at her and gestured for her to come stand next to me.

"How'd you sleep?"

"Fine," she replied. "There's something about being away from home… I didn't wake up once all night."

I smiled. "Good. Glad to hear it. Did you have anything to eat yet?"

"No, not yet." Fiona looked out towards the bay as she answered me. A steady breeze rustled her hair.

"Well, you better grab something. We've got to leave in an hour."

"Oh?" she said, as she turned to face me. "I thought we had a bit of down time for a couple of days."

"We do. This isn't work-related."

Before she could reply, I pointed in the direction of the bay towards the sailboats.

"See that?"

Fiona swiveled her head and followed the line of my finger. "See what?"

"The sailboats."

"Yes. What about them?"

"That's what we're doing today. Just you and me. We're going sailing."

All of sudden, Fiona showed me the back of her head as she broke her gaze on the bay. She began to walk away from me and I studied her as she moved. The boards of the veranda creaked a bit as she stepped until at last, she stopped, about ten feet away. Grabbing my coffee cup, I made my way over to her.

After taking a sip of the smoky blackness, I closed to within a few feet of her.

"Something the matter?"

"I-I can't go on a sailboat, Gabe."

"Why? Are you afraid you're going to fall overboard and drown?"

"Something like that."

I wrinkled my brow and made my away around in front of Fiona. As she came into view, I noticed she'd started to spin the gems on her bracelet back and forth. I watched for a couple of moments, and after another gulp of the bitter dark liquid, I spoke once again.

"Wanna talk about it?"

"No," she said with a whisper.

As Fiona finished her thought, she attempted to walk past me. I stepped in front of her, blocking her path.

"Gabe please…"

"What? What's going on with you Fiona? Why are you afraid of the water… going sailing?"

She tilted her head upwards, and as her eyes came into view, I noticed they held a thick gloss in them. A fraction of a second later, tears began to flow. Fiona's lips curled upward, and before I realized it, she crushed herself into me. As she sobbed, uncontrollable jerks of her shoulders and pulses of her torso shook her. I slid my arms around her upper body, holding her with a tender, but firm embrace.

We stood there in silence for the better part of a minute as she wept. I did my best to comfort her, but she seemed to be inconsolable. Her body shuddered as wave after wave of emotion ripped through her. The nearby canopy echoed with the sounds of her wails and moans until at last, I moved my hands to her shoulders and leaned away from her.

"Fiona. What is wrong? Was it something I said?"

Red-eyed and puffy cheeked, Fiona looked up at me through a sheen of grief. She shook her head. "N-No. I-It's n-not you, Gabe. I-I'm sorry."

"Don't worry about it, Fiona. Whatever it is you can tell me."

She shook her head again. "N-No, I-I can't. I can't. I can't…"

I glanced down at her bracelet once more. "I noticed you touched that just before you started to cry. What's with the charm bracelet, Fiona?"

Fiona made two quick swipes across her face, erasing the tears as she did. After a sniffle, she stood tall and grew stone-faced.

"Gabe, please. I asked you politely. I don't want to talk about it, okay? I'm sorry for behaving like that."

I shook my head at her sudden obstinacy. "Okay, Fiona. I won't press you on it. I'm going to get ready."

With that, I turned and began to walk away. As I did, Fiona cleared her throat. "Where are you going?"

I stopped and did half-turn, looking at her over my shoulder. "Sailing. Remember?"

"Oh," she said with a nod. "Right."

I looked at her for a moment before turning away again and heading inside. But, I hadn't gotten more than a foot or two before she spoke up once more.

"Gabe, wait."

I paused and pivoted until I faced her. "What?"

Fiona drew her hands together in front of her body and started to walk in my direction. The entire time, she kept her head down and clutched her charm bracelet until she stopped about a foot away.

After she did, she reached up and pulled her hair behind her ears. In the distance, the whistles of a dozen forest-dwelling birds filled the air with a symphony of chirps. The energetic tone of their sounds stood in sharp contrast to the somber look on Fiona's face as she looked into my eyes.

"I… I've never told anyone this before."

I nodded, but didn't respond.

She groaned, seeming as if a sudden jolt of doubt hit her.

"Okay, okay," she began, as she raised her hands, showing me her palms. "I'm just going to tell you."

"All right."

"The reason I'm terrified of the water... It has nothing to do with being afraid to drown, okay?"

"Okay."

"Um, see... When I was ten years old, we went on a family vacation. My mom, Dad, two brothers, my grandmother and me. We always went to the beach on vacations. Believe it or not, I used to love the water. But I don't anymore, not since that vacation."

I felt a hollowness hit my gut. There was no question in my mind as to how this story would end. I interrupted her.

"Fiona, you don't have to do this. It's okay. Really. If you don't want to go with me, it's fine."

"No, Gabe," she replied right away. As she spoke, I noticed her demeanor change once again. Still sad, she seemed stoic and determined. "I want to tell you. I trust you."

"All right, Fiona."

Fiona then proceeded to recount the horror of the summer vacation that took the lives of her entire family. They'd apparently gone sailing when the vessel capsized at the whim of what investigators expected was a rogue wave. The life jackets were still on board. It was more than eight hours before the first rescue team arrived, and by then, it was too late.

They'd all drowned.

Apparently Fiona had fractured her arm a couple of days before and had been unable to go and had instead, stayed behind, cared for by her grandmother. Through gulps of grief and swaths of tears, she concluded the story by lifting the arm with the charm bracelet on it.

"M-My grandmother gave this to me not long after," she said. Fiona gestured towards the stones, telling me the lost family member each represented. "I-I've had to get a larger bracelet as the years have gone on, of course, but remember when you asked me at the bar about it?"

I smiled at her. "Of course."

Fiona paused for a moment to collect herself. With a succession of wipes across her cheeks, she exhaled and continued.

"Well, I lied to you, obviously, when I said it didn't mean anything to me. It means *everything*. I'm sorry I wasn't truthful."

"Fiona, don't even worry about it," I said, as I stepped towards her. "Look, I… I feel like shit. Hell, if I'd known about this, I never would have suggested we go sailing in the first place."

"It's okay, Gabe. There's no way you could have known. You don't have to apologize. I'm grateful for the offer, though."

It was one thing to know about their deaths ahead of time but I hadn't meant to hurt her in the process. Maybe that was a bit of karma coming back at me for checking on her in the first place. Even so, that's a risk I had to take at the time. The simple fact was, I wouldn't have done anything different.

Still, I couldn't help but feel bad for her.

"Look, Fiona," I began, nodding in the direction of the bay. "I'm gonna skip sailing. We'll do something else."

Fiona's eyes widened. "No, no, Gabe. Please don't do that. I want you to go sailing if you want to. Just…"

I tented my eyebrows with an expectant look. "Just… what?"

"Promise me you'll stay close to the bay."

I chuckled. "Fiona, I happen to be an expert swimmer. I was captain of my college swim team. Not only that, but I've been a certified diver since I was a teenager, and I've also done my fair share of free diving."

Still not swayed, Fiona blinked. "What's free diving?"

"The same thing as scuba, except with no oxygen tanks," I replied. For emphasis, I tapped against my chest. "It's all about the lungs, and I've got some of the best."

"Oh."

I turned towards the bay and gestured up towards the clear skies overhead. "Besides, there's not a cloud in the sky. Look at the water, Fiona. There's hardly any wave action. Nothing is going to go wrong."

"Hmm," she grumbled. "Well, okay. But, please be careful."

"Come with me," I said, with a hint of a challenge in my tone.

Fiona's eyes widened once again. "No. Oh no, Gabe. I-I couldn't."

I stepped close to Fiona. Reaching down, I cradled her upper arms. "Fiona. You're a rational person. You have to know that what happened to your family... It's not going to happen out in that bay. There's not going to be any rogue waves. You've made so many strides in recent months. What better time than right now to confront your fear?"

Fiona turned her head and swallowed hard as she glanced in the direction of the aquamarine water. But almost as soon, she snapped her head in my direction again.

"Gabe, I can't," she said. Lifting her arms, Fiona held her hands up in front of her face. "I mean, look at me. I'm trembling just thinking about it."

I released my grip from her shoulders and swallowed her shaky hands with my fingers. I held her there for a moment, until she calmed down and looked me in the eye.

"Fiona, I'm not going to *make you* do it. All right? But, I think you should. For yourself."

She remained silent and looked up at me as I paused.

"I promise. *Nothing* will go wrong. At its deepest, the water in the bay is not more than twenty feet. We'll put two life jackets on you and cover the lengths of both your arms and legs with water wings. You'll be unsinkable."

Fiona arched an eyebrow at me. "Hah, hah. I can swim, Gabe. That's not the point."

"Okay then, so whatd'ya say? Let's give it a shot."

As soon as I finished speaking, Fiona sucked in her lower lip and began to chew on it. While she did, I extended my hand in her direction, offering it to her.

"Come on."

FIONA

I followed Gabe back inside the suite. As I entered, he made his way across the room towards the kitchen.

"We need to get some food in you, Fiona." He paused and looked at me for a moment. "And I think a mimosa might be in order as well."

Exhausted from what had just transpired on the veranda, I dragged myself towards the kitchen.

"I don't want anything to drink, Gabe. It's not even ten o'clock in the morning yet."

"Don't be ridiculous," Gabe said, as he came around the corner and slid his hand against my lower back. He leaned in and placed a tender kiss on my cheek. "You're on vacation today, Fiona, remember? There are no clocks."

As he spoke, I plopped down on one of the nearby stools lining the opposite side of the kitchen countertop. Semi-slumped, I exhaled and dropped my hands in my lap. Gabe nodded as I turned and looked at him.

"I'll make it a double," he said.

For a half a second, I almost protested, but before I could, Gabe headed towards the refrigerator. I watched as he pulled out a bottle of champagne and a pitcher of orange juice. With a kick from his heel, Gabe closed the door and walked back towards me. Less than a minute later, he'd poured us a couple of glasses.

Passing one to me, he raised his.

"How about a toast?"

I shrugged. I wasn't exactly in the toasting mood.

"Ah, come on now, Fiona. Cheer up. Look where you are! A beautiful island, hidden away from everyone, with the world's most handsome bartender at your service."

I looked up at him. A small grin came to my lips.

"Now see!" he exclaimed. "That's more like it. How about that toast?"

"Okay. Well, what do you want to toast to?"

Without hesitating, Gabe continued. "I'd like to toast to you, Fiona. To your beauty, your strength and your courage."

"Oh," I muttered as he spoke. "I really don't think…"

Gabe interrupted me. "Just shut up and drink the damn drink, woman."

With that, he angled the long, slender flute in my direction. I smiled once more and did the same, *clinking* my glass into his. After a healthy swig, I closed my eyes as the alcohol-filled citrus rolled across my taste buds and slid down my throat.

It tasted so good—so good I took another sip right away. The cold of the cocktail stood in perfect contrast to the air inside the suite, made warm by the ever-present ocean breeze circulating about. Nearly half gone after only two sips, the drink sloshed a bit as I placed the glass on the countertop.

"Wow," Gabe began. "For someone who doesn't like to drink first thing in the morning that sure went down quick."

Just then, he lifted the champagne bottle and offered to pour some more for me. Shaking my head, I slid my hand over the top of the glass.

"No thank you. If I drink any more than that, you'll have to carry me to the boat."

Gabe nodded. "Yeah, come to think of it, that's probably a good idea. Let's get you something to eat."

"Okay," I replied. "But not too much."

Over the next several minutes I looked on in disbelief as Gabe made his way around the kitchen as easily as he did the boardroom. Without missing a beat, he cracked eggs, fried bacon and toasted bread to perfection. All the while he continued to sell me on the idea of the sailboat.

Even with the alcohol kicking in, I still had huge reservations about the excursion. But watching him at work soothed me in a way I couldn't explain. It was as if nothing was beyond his capacity to accomplish… even something as simple as bacon and eggs.

"Here ya go," he said, as he slid the plate across the counter.

It came to a spinning stop, directly beneath my face. I looked down at the perfectly round, sunny-side up eggs, crispy bacon and lightly buttered toast, arranged as if it were prepared at a five-star restaurant. I took another pull of my near-empty mimosa.

"I am… wow."

Gabe flung the kitchen towel over his shoulder. "What? What's wrong?"

I looked up at him. "Wrong? No, nothing's wrong. Where did you learn to cook like this? As breakfasts go, this is about the most appetizing I've ever seen."

Gabe nodded. "Wait 'til you taste it."

"Really?"

Gabe frowned. "No, Fiona, I made you breakfast so you could admire it. You want me to get your phone so you can take pictures of it also?"

"What?"

"Oh Jesus, nothing," Gabe said, as he pointed at the plate. "Just eat, would ya?"

After a few bites, I had to admit he'd blown me away. The eggs were a delight, the bacon salty, with just the right amount of crisp… and the way he prepared the toast… Adding anything to it besides butter would have been a crime.

"Well?" he said, as I swallowed a bite.

"Gabe, it's… delicious. Where did you learn to cook?"

Gabe leaned against the counter. "When I was in college, all four years of undergrad, I worked the night shift as the short-order cook at a greasy spoon downtown. It's good, right?"

In all the long hours I'd worked on the Link Protocol with Gabe, I don't think I'd ever seen him beam with the kind of pride he displayed in that moment. As much as I hated to admit it, it had been easy for me to forget Gabe hadn't always been the man who stood before me today. He'd come up the hard way, fighting for his success every step along the way.

I had the distinct feeling that as he smiled at me, he was every bit as proud of the breakfast he'd made, if not more so, than the hundreds of billions he stood to make on the Link Protocol. Just then, I realized I'd sat there in admiration of him for a few moments too long.

"What's wrong?" he said, as he leaned away from me. Disappointment creased his brow.

I sat forward in a hurry, snapping myself out of it.

"N-No," I stammered, as I searched my mind for an appropriate lie. "I was just thinking about the sailing trip again. I'm sorry, Gabe. It is… well, it's the best breakfast I've ever eaten. What more can I say?"

Gabe nodded his head and smiled. "Good. I'm glad you like it."

FIONA

Just as he finished speaking, Gabe leaned in and kissed me, sliding his hand behind my head as he did. Although I probably should have expected it and resisted, the simple fact was he'd caught me by surprise and I didn't.

It was such a beautiful place and the truth was that I was tired. In reality, nothing would have felt better than the satin-like feel of his lips against mine just then. I relented and leaned into Gabe, giving in to his strength and my need for it. Without a word, he separated his lips from mine.

"Give me your hand," he said.

Still in a daze from our kiss, I did as he asked. "Why?"

"Well, Fiona, we have to shower," he began, as he tugged at me, pulling me off the stool. "You can't get in the ocean dirty. That just wouldn't be polite."

"Oh, I see."

Within minutes, Gabe stripped away what resistance I pretended to still have, and, after starting the shower, he reached down and grabbed hold of the door handle, tugging it open. Trailing Gabe's chiseled backside into the heated mist, I watched as he walked under one of two large showerheads.

I closed on him just as the rain from overhead slid down his magnificent torso. Rivulets of wet heat rippled along his hard frame as I drew near, rubbing my body against his like a forlorn kitten.

I looked up into Gabe's eyes, and as I did he leaned down and kissed me with a single, soft press against my cheek. Chills raced along my spine as he moved closer and trailed his slick lips down the side of my neck.

I trembled as Gabe's tongue and lips suckled my wet flesh. Just then, he reached up and pulled my hair out of his way. With a tender slap, it clung to my back as Gabe's mouth moved around behind me to the center of my neck, just above my shoulder blades.

My head listed and rocked like a wayward sea vessel in the midst of a storm. As the shower rained heat upon me, I leaned my curves against him. Gabe's hands raced towards my hips, where he grabbed them and squeezed firmly. My lips parted, and as they did, a few droplets made their way inside. I tasted the water, laced with Gabe's essence. A heady mix of musk and sweat rolled across my tongue like a subtle wave laps against a dock.

Gabe's hands made their way around from my hips to my belly, just above the waist, where he held them still for a moment. I stretched my arms up as he moved ever closer. My hands traveled along the outside of his thick forearms, rounded biceps and all the way up to his broad, dripping wet shoulders. Turning away from him for an instant, my head fell into his chest, my back pressed against his torso and my ass into his engorged cock.

Breath hitched in my throat when I bumped against it, but as I did, Gabe held me firm. He groaned as I brushed the curve of my rear along his long, hard dick. Just then, I tilted my head back and invited him towards my mouth. A split second later, Gabe's tongue slipped inside, and as it did, I reached down with my hand and wrapped it around base of his cock.

I began to roll my hand and make long, slow pulls up the length of his shaft. Our kisses intensified as Gabe's hands made their way along the midline of my torso until my tits fell into them. He groped and squeezed at them while I continued to stroke him, my grip lubricated by the hot water as it rained down from overhead.

I moaned as Gabe rolled my nipples between the tips of his fingers. As the seconds ticked by, my lower back started to arch, and my breasts heaved upward, eager for more of his touch. By now, my nipples were hardened under the firmness of his grasp and the incessant flow of water across them. At last, our lips broke apart and a gap in the water flow provided me a wisp of cool air.

Whether from the heat of the shower or Gabe's body pressed into mine, I started to feel light headed. As if he sensed it, Gabe dropped his hands away from my breasts and swept me into his arms. Now face-to-face, I felt the hot tease of his breath upon my lips once again. My hands wrapped around his broad upper body as he moved with ease across the tile floor. Moments later, he sank down to his knees and placed me down upon a long marble ledge.

A second shower head poured down on the stone as I positioned myself. The heat from the wet marble felt good against my backside. My limbs went limp as I relaxed into the warmth and the power of Gabe's affection. It was all I could do to prop myself up on my elbows, just in time to see him kneel in front of me. Slack-jawed, I gazed down between my legs as Gabe spread them apart. Heated liquid poured down over me and ran like an overwhelmed stream bank towards my pussy.

Gabe flipped his head back and as he did, his hair flashed a wave of spray in every direction. Half-dazed, I watched as he opened his mouth. Water from above rained into it until at last, he leaned forward and lowered his head towards my exposed, pink flesh. A mischievous grin crept to the edges of his lips as he reached up and placed his hands in the center of my thighs.

Water ricocheted off my hardened nipples as he broke eye contact with me and started to descend. My breath came in rapid gulps, in fits of anticipation and need. And then, he revealed the purpose to his actions from moments before when he drove straight into the center of my thighs. Without warning, his mouth pressed hard into it and as it did, he released a heated flood of water along my folds.

I cried out in pleasure as his tongue moved along the center of my slit. Gabe continued to pulse a steady stream of water as my hips shook in his hands. My head bobbed up and down as he consumed me, when just a few seconds later, the suction from his lips broke free.

I glanced up to see that once more he held his head back as water poured inside. His knees squeaked on the tile and echoed along the walls of the steamed-up space as he filled up his mouth. With almost no time for me to recover, Gabe's head descended between my thighs yet again. His lips pressed into me as before and the water he concealed within his mouth spilled out. Gabe's tongue delved within me and then curled back towards him, beckoning my climax with each hot, fluid-filled, flick.

I writhed on the marble like a trapped animal, but without thinking, I angled my hips upwards towards his mouth. Gabe's hands slipped beneath my ass as he delivered the final hot jets of water inside me. My entire body quaked and vibrated. Unable or unwilling to control the primal urge scratching at me from deep inside, I reached up and grabbed two fistfuls of Gabe's hair as he licked and sucked me with feverish intent.

"Ohhh, ohhh, ohhh," I moaned.

My hips locked, cemented in place by the flow of desire that bubbled deep within my core. I curled my fingers in his thick locks until I felt the tips of them reach the tenderness of his scalp. The moment grew too big for me to try and hold back, to hang on for just one more instant of slow gratification.

Instead, I cried out…

"I'm cumming… ahhh… ahhh… ahhh!!!"

My body suffered in delight under the deluge of my first water-induced orgasm. Gabe held me in place but allowed my mind the freedom to drift down the stream of bliss. For several seconds, I moved my hips in slow, round circles grinding my pussy against his mouth, until at last I felt it too sensitive to continue, and with a whisper, I begged him for a respite.

In the immediate afterglow, I looked at Gabe as water from the large shower head peppered his spectacular V-shaped torso. I dragged my fingertips along my body and up towards my breasts, where I paused and squeezed them together.

Just then, Gabe began to rise to his feet. I lay naked before him, exposed like never before and eager to see what would happen next. Using the shower's rain as my guide, I allowed my eyes to wander all the way down his chiseled body, until his prodigious gift filled my vision.

I motioned to Gabe with my index finger and within seconds he moved towards my lips. He lingered there for a moment and as he did, my eyes fluttered closed. Gabe's mouth pressed into mine and his tongue wasted no time in making its claim. He invaded me with passion and kissed like he meant for me never to forget it. With my head flat against the marble, I angled my mouth up towards his and beckoned him to take all that he cared to and do so with no qualms.

Just then, Gabe grabbed my ankles and pulled me to the precipice of the ledge. My backside slid and squeaked along the marble until my movement stopped and my ass cheeks bumped against Gabe's powerful thighs. As it did, Gabe leaned his thighs into my legs and pressed the immense bulge of his cock into the outermost edges of my folds.

My pussy lips wrapped around it around like a wild jungle plant. A primal ferocity gripped at me in that moment and it took all my willpower not to reach down and pull him inside myself. Literally, my hand shook with the desire to do it.

Yet, instead of giving me what I yearned for, he gave me what he wanted and began drag the thick tip up and down the length of my pussy. I moaned, cocooned in tortuous pleasure, as Gabe used his cock like a tuning fork and primed me for the instant he'd give his virtuoso performance upon me. He paused long enough for me to notice and then, with a single swift motion, delivered the full measure of his manhood.

Within seconds, deep, steady blows pulsed in and out of my pussy. With each pass of his shaft between the tight confines of my folds, I shook with pleasure. Inch by tortuous inch, Gabe claimed every bit of me.

Under the steady warmth of the rain above, I felt once more as if I were in service to him… *lost to him*. As Gabe slid his wet, hard cock in and out, I felt worshipped. Every grunt from him was a primal tribute to my femininity, every moan a visceral desire to have me all to himself, in every way. My ears filled with sounds of our passion and amid the pillows of steam, I began to feel us melt into one.

"Mmm, hmm…" I moaned, as Gabe fucked me. "Mmm, hmm…"

And then, without warning, Gabe's cadence changed from steady thrusts to a slow, syrupy pulse. The sensation drove me mad. Over and again, Gabe inserted the full measure of his dick inside me, as deep as it would go, until the thick head bumped against my insides. After a brief pause, he would reverse the motion and move it almost all the way back out, leaving only the tip inside me.

I cooed while I reached down towards him. His hands grasped me at the hips, and as I grabbed hold of his dense forearms, he peered down at me. I offered a lustful smile as our eyes met, but Gabe did not return it.

Instead, as water licked and rolled across his square jaw, he stared back at me with a sexually threatening gaze. My breath escaped through a small part in my lips just as he yanked me towards him once more. Startled, I dug my nails into his forearms and moaned as he entered into my depths like never before.

Where moments earlier he tantalized me with control and restraint, now he riveted my attention with the opposite. Gabe angled his torso over me and placed his right palm in the center of my belly. He thrust with recklessness and pinned me to the marble beneath, as all the while my supple flesh rippled in waves of submission.

I rocked back and forth as his frenetic pace continued, and as it did, I dug my heels into his rock-hard ass and pulled. My senses told me his moment was near. I didn't want there to be any chance I wouldn't be prepared to receive all he had to offer.

And offer it he would, for in the next few seconds, Gabe flung his head back.

Spray from his wet hair flashed in every direction once again and he stared up at the ceiling for an instant before returning his attention to me. I felt his ass cheeks draw inward with a hard pull and stop.

A deep guttural moan rumbled in his abdomen, made its way up through his throat and spilled out of his mouth in the form of an emphatic growl. His upper torso lurched forward while at the same instant he began to thrust inside of me with renewed fervor. I gripped at his forearms, made slick by his effort and the ever-present shower steam.

Gabe's entire body flexed and bowed as he neared the moment of his climax. Just then, I felt a series of small tremors build, followed next by the deepest and most forceful thrusts yet. Gabe grunted and with a final push, drove the entire length of his cock inside me.

"Aaaaaaahhhhhh!!!!!" he yelled as he fell forward over my midsection.

And then, in the next instant, he erupted. Hot ejaculate laced me as his cock descended into my deepest of places. I reached up and clawed his hard backside as orgasm gripped at his body. His dick buried to the hilt, Gabe held it there as jet after jet slipped within me. I raked my nails across his back, and as I did, his head reared up. A twisted mix of pain and pleasure folded his face in delight as the swan song of his ecstasy approached.

For a few more seconds, he held there, connecting us in bliss. When at last it began to recede, he leaned over and kissed me. As we separated, he helped me to my feet and moved back towards the center of the shower. He soaped and shampooed me from head to toe for at least ten minutes, if not more.

As we finished, Gabe offered me a towel.

"So," he began. "Ready to go sailing?"

FIONA

Gabe captained the boat to a spot just beyond the edge of the bay.

"I thought you said we were staying closer to shore."

He winked at me. "Just getting a bit of privacy. Don't worry, we'll be fine."

As he finished, Gabe tossed the boat's anchor overboard. I wasn't pleased with his response nor the fact that we were beyond the confines of the bay. In fact, the water was quite choppy and as the anchor sank to the bottom, I grabbed onto the edge of my seat.

"You okay?" Gabe said, as he turned back towards me.

"No! I'm mad at you. You told me we were staying in the bay. And now look! We're out here with the waves and everything."

Gabe stood from where he sat and made his way towards me. After a moment or two, he squatted down next to me.

"Fiona. Everything is fine, all right? Look, it's a glorious day out. You don't have to worry about the waves. They aren't more than a foot high at the most. Just think of it as if you're in your car driving down a rolling road. It's no different."

As he spoke, I sensed my death grip ease a bit.

"Here, look," he began, turning his back and gesturing towards the clear blue water just beyond the side of the boat.

I didn't budge. After a few moments, Gabe reached towards me and folded his fingers around my forearm. "Come on, Fiona. Come look."

I didn't stand, but instead scooted down the length of my seat in his direction. When I got close enough to the edge to see the water, I stopped in place.

"This is as far as I go. Right here."

Gabe shook his head and chuckled. "Okay. Well, I guess you can still see from there."

"See what?"

Over the next several minutes, Gabe pointed out at least a dozen different kinds of fish as they swam by the sailboat. As he spoke, the sun's rays licked at my skin. The warmth settled me a bit.

Just then, a salt-filled gust of sea air floated past my nostrils, and combined with the gentle laps of water against the side of the boat, it helped my edginess begin to dissipate further. Feeling a bit more at ease, I edged closer to the end of my seat, so much so that by the time Gabe turned around once again, I was within inches of him.

"Oh, hey," he said with hint of surprise in his tone. "Glad you could join me."

I grimaced at him.

"A barracuda!" he said, pointing towards the water. "Fiona, have a look. He's a monster."

With one hand pressed into the middle of Gabe's back, I leaned forward, peering over the side. As I did, a long slender fish, pulsed by, swatting its tail back and forth with precision. It shined and shimmered, looking as if it were made of chrome, as the sun's rays reflected down on it.

Just then, Gabe pointed to his right. "Another one!"

I turned my head to look, and a splash of water from a passing swell coated my face. The saltwater burned my eyes, and as I reached up to rub them, my hand collided with Gabe's. I felt my charm bracelet catch on his wristwatch and then a split second later, I sensed it vanish from my wrist with sickening snap.

With eyes full of salt, I opened them as much as I could and screamed, "My bracelet!"

Gabe hadn't realized he'd done anything.

"What?" he replied with a tone of confusion in his voice.

Rubbing my eyes as hard as I could, I yelled, "My bracelet it… it got caught on your watch and snapped free!"

"Oh shit!" Gabe began. As I continued to try and rid my eyes of the salt, I heard Gabe clamor about the inside of the sailboat. Several 'um's' and 'ah's' later, he'd verified my worst fears.

"I don't see it, Fiona. It must have gone over the side."

"What?!" I screamed, as I flipped my eyes open at last. The terror that glued me to my seat moments before left my body as I dove towards the side of the boat, looking over it in desperation. The entire vessel listed and Gabe lost his balance, nearly falling on top of me as a result.

"Jesus, Fiona!" he exclaimed. "Be careful!"

"My bracelet!" I cried out, ignoring him. "It's gone!"

"No," Gabe replied, without a moment's hesitation. "We can get it. Just gotta go in after it."

Still overwhelmed by the loss, I only half-listened to him as he began to strip away his clothing, starting with his shirt. Slack-jawed, I stared into the water in utter despair. I'd had that bracelet for more than half my life and now, in a fraction of a second, it was gone. It was as if I'd lost my family all over again in a twist of horrifying irony.

Yet, the entire time I gawked at the passing swells, Gabe continued to remove his clothes, finally kicking off his flip flops. At last, still half-dazed, I turned my head in his direction.

"What are you doing?"

Gabe frowned as if I'd asked him the dumbest question imaginable.

"What do you mean?" he scoffed. "I'm going in after it."

I shook my head, "No, no, no. Gabe, please don't."

Yet within a second or two, Gabe looked as if he was about to jump in.

"Wait..." I said, as another surge of adrenaline hit me. "How long can you hold your breath underwater?"

"A couple of minutes. Why?"

"Ohh, I don't know. I just... Gabe, I hate this."

"Well we don't really have a choice do we, Fiona? If a barracuda happens to see your bracelet sailing towards the bottom, it'll snatch it up and it will be gone forever. They are attracted to shiny objects. Is that what you want?"

"No, of course it isn't, but... I'm worried about you. What if something happens?"

Gabe took a quick seat across from me, jarring the boat and causing it to rock from side-to-side.

"Gabe!" I shrieked, as I grabbed on to my seat with every ounce of strength I had. "Please be careful!"

Gabe ignored me and instead grabbed me by the forearms and pried my fingers loose from the seat beneath me. He brought my hands around in front of my body and folded his fingers over mine. My frantic breath slowed a bit as he held me there for a moment or two before he started to speak.

"Fiona, you need to calm down right now. Okay?"

My mouth was so dry, I couldn't force down a single swallow. I nodded.

"Here's what's going to happen. I'm going to search for your bracelet, get it, and then bring it back. Understand?"

A million scenarios jumbled in my mind. Nearly all of them wound up with him dead. As I sat there fretting, Gabe stood. It was as if time slowed Gabe's movement as I watched him. And then, without so much as another word or a look in my direction, Gabe jumped off the side of the sailboat, arching into the water as if he'd been born to do it.

Thinking quickly, I reached for my beach bag and pulled out my cell phone. An urge to time how long he'd been submerged overwhelmed me. My hands trembled as I groped inside and felt around for it.

"Oh come on…" I groaned at last. Yanking the bag up near my face for a better view, I finally spotted it. Without wasting a second, I grabbed it, swiped it on, and opened the timer app. As I did, I glanced over the side of the boat. I estimated he'd been under for at least fifteen seconds at this point.

"Okay, add fifteen," I muttered as I started the timer.

As soon as I did, I returned my attention over the side and waited. It wasn't long before I'd reached an estimated thirty seconds, then forty-five, then sixty. I inched forward, peering over the side of the boat.

Even though the water was clear, I could only see down about ten feet or so. Gabe said it was at last twenty feet in this spot so straining to see much further probably wouldn't do me any good.

At one minute, fifteen seconds, my stomach sank.

Glancing at the timer, I muttered, "Gabe, what the hell are you doing?"

Where the hell was he? *Oh my God. Oh my God.*

But just as I'd reached a state of near paralysis, I heard a splashing sound to my right. Just then Gabe surfaced, thrashing his head and slinging his long wet hair away from his eyes.

"Gabe!" I screamed. "Oh, my God!"

As I spoke, Gabe started to swim back in the direction of the boat. Soon enough, he arrived and gripped onto the side with his fingers.

"You had me worried sick!" I said.

Gabe laughed. "You seem pissed right now."

"That's because I am pissed! I thought you drowned!"

"Okay, okay…" Gabe replied, interrupting me. "Calm down. I'm fine. No luck yet, though. Just came up to grab air, then I'll go back."

"What!" I exclaimed. "No, Gabe. No! I don't care about the bracelet. I don't want anything to happen to you. Please. Just get back in the boat."

"Aww," Gabe said with a wink and ill-timed smirk. "So you do care. Huh, Fiona?"

I thinned my lips at him. "I'm not in the mood, Gabe. Please just get in the boat with me."

Gabe shook his head and pushed himself away from the side. The movement of his body created a small wake around his upper torso, swallowing it in foamy blue.

"Back in a minute, babe."

"Gabe! No!"

But before I could get a second word out, I lost sight of him as the last part to submerge, his toes, vanished beneath the water's surface. I glanced around the immediate area as soon as Gabe disappeared from view.

"Where the hell did everyone go?" I stammered. "Where are all the boats?"

In fact, as I scanned the entire area, I didn't see a single living soul. What the hell was I going to do if something happened to him?

Before I realized it, nearly the same length of time Gabe had been down before passed by once again. With each second past the time when he ought to have resurfaced, I fretted.

Nearly to the point of panic, I stood in the boat, reaching above my head and grasping the sail to steady myself. I traced the top of the water, following each whitecap as it dissipated into foam.

"Gabe!" I screamed. "Gabe!"

All of a sudden, from behind, I heard the sound of a great gasp for air. Spinning in place, I caught Gabe as he surfaced once more. I scrambled across the boat to the other side and knelt down near the edge. Gabe gulped for breath as he swam back up to the boat.

"Gabe, please," I begged. "You are *terrifying* me. Please, just forget about the bracelet okay? I'm begging you."

Gabe heaved several more breaths.

"Fiona… Don't… Worry… About it."

"Well I am going to worry about it. I don't want you risking your life over it. This is crazy! Please get back in the boat."

Gabe shook his head. "I think I know… where… it went. There's a huge patch of sand… down there. There's nothing covering… any of it. I'm gonna go look."

I felt tears begin to well up in my eyes. "Gabe, no. Please don't, I…"

But as I begged, Gabe's head vanished beneath the surface once again as he submerged.

"Goddamnit!" I yelled, slamming my hand on the seat beneath me.

Enraged and filled with dread, I reached for my cell phone once more and started the timer. By now, I'd grown accustomed to Gabe being submerged for a couple of minutes at least, so unless a passing shark decided to have an early lunch, I assumed he'd be back.

With that, a sudden wave of exhaustion came over me. I placed my phone down next to me, and after propping my elbows on my knees, I dropped my head into my hands. I tried to calm myself, taking a number of deep breaths. After several inhales and exhales, the muscles in my neck and upper back began to relax a bit.

After a final exhale, I licked the salt air from my lips and lifted my head up. My hair hung in front of my eyes for a moment, and as it did, streaks from the sun flickered amid the strands. I blew a puff of tension out from between my lips and pulled the strands back behind my ears, clearing my line of sight.

Just then, I turned a bit and reached for my phone. Flipping it over, I did a double take when I noticed the time... *three minutes and nineteen seconds!* The calm that had descended upon me stripped away, as panic once again took its place.

"Oh shit!" I said, as I lurched towards the side of the boat nearest to me.

For several anxious seconds, I scanned the surface of the water as I had twice before, but I didn't see any sign of Gabe. Frantic, I scooted across to the opposite side, hoping he might appear there, as he had the last time. As before, I glued my eyes to the undulating currents and subtle whitecaps.

Oh my God. Oh my God. Oh my God!

He'd never stayed down this long before. What if something happened to him? What if he'd gotten attacked or worse, what if he was trapped on the bottom somehow? I grabbed my phone once more.

Almost four minutes!

Without another thought, I stood and began to strip my clothing away. I'd never been so terrified in my life, but I wasn't about to lose him... not like this. Overwhelmed with fear, I ambled to the side of the boat, taking one last peek over the side as I did.

I had no idea where to even begin looking for him, but as the seconds raced by, I realized I had no choice but to take the risk. If I didn't, Gabe could die and I'd never be able to live with myself.

I grabbed hold of the railing on the side of the boat, and my hands shook so much they vibrated. I groped at railing, hoping for a moment of clarity, and after a quick prayer, I began the countdown.

"Okay Fiona, on the count of three. Three… Two… One…"

Slipperless Series

(Book #3)

Copyright 2015 by Sloan Storm

All rights reserved. This book or any portion thereof may not be reproduced or used in any manner whatsoever without the express written permission of the author or publisher except for the use of brief quotations in critical articles or reviews.

Made in the USA
San Bernardino, CA
30 December 2015